I0557632

Where We May Wag

Writing Piazza Press

Where We May Wag
Copyright © 2018 Kara Piazza
All rights reserved.

No portion of this work may be reproduced in print or electronically, other than brief excerpts for the purpose of reviews, without permission of the publisher.

This book is a work of fiction. All the characters, names, and places, incidents, and dialogue in this anthology are either products of the author's imagination or used fictitiously. Any resemblance to actual persons, places, and events is coincidental.

Writing Piazza Press
thewritingpiazza@gmail.com
Library of Congress Cataloging-in-Publication Data Available

ISBN: 0-9969883-2-7
ISBN–13: 978-09969883-2-2

Contents

Acknowledgments

Foremost, we couldn't have put this anthology together without the patience and flexibility of our many authors. This collection has been a long time coming, and we've met with plenty of support and excitement despite our sometimes lengthy pauses along the way. Thanks to Wikimedia Commons for the public domain images accompanying each story. We're also grateful to Horror Tree and Dark Markets for getting the word out there and encouraging submissions.

Thanks also to our readers. It is those people we most want to reach, those who have perhaps a mere curiosity about animal testing and its consequences. Hopefully these stories will inspire change, encourage further investigation, and add perspective on what so many creatures endure to this day.

If They Catch Me

by Kara Piazza

If they catch me, I'll go to jail.

I tugged at my dark clothing, which felt strange through my black leather gloves. My ensemble was meant to make me blend into the night, but instead the outfit made it feel like I had the words "criminal activity eminent" written all over me in DayGlo colors. I used to be such a good girl, now look at me. I sighed.

Straight to jail.... Well, juvie. Maybe I could get it expunged after I turn eighteen. Maybe they'll go easy on me since it's my first offense. My first offense! Why am I assuming they'll catch me? Maybe they won't.

My thoughts tumbled over one another. I used my sleeve to wipe the sweat from my forehead and took some deep breaths to try to slow my racing thoughts.

"Hey. What are you doing?"

The whispered question made me jump high enough that both of my feet left the ground. My heart only started beating again sometime after I landed.

"Geez, Gabe, you can't sneak up on people like that," I hissed.

"Sorry Summer, but if you don't want to be snuck up on, you shouldn't be sneaking through the night dressed like a ninja." Gabe chuckled softly.

"How did you even know I was here? Did you follow me?" My eyes darted around, making sure I hadn't missed anyone else in the area. I didn't see his car anywhere. I turned back to face him with a frown.

"Yeah, I saw you climb out your window. I just had to know what could get *you* to sneak out of the house. Nothing

I ever suggested was good enough to warrant such rebellion." His lips quirked up at the corners.

"I'm just looking around." I edged towards a hodge-podge of buildings.

"Riiiiight." He moved when I moved.

I scanned the building ledges.

"Do you see any cameras?" I asked, without tearing my eyes away from the search.

Gabe turned his focus to the buildings. He squinted and surveyed the buildings just as I had. "I don't see any back here, why? Should there be?" He frowned.

"I guess their animal torturing budget didn't include security costs." The venom in my voice was so thick I felt as though I could chew it.

Gabe's mouth dropped open, and his eyes grew wide. I sighed and moved toward the outcrop of buildings. I left the tall grass along the bank of the river and moved to cross the road. I glanced back in the direction I had left my car but couldn't see it from here. I'd parked a ways away.

"Animal torturing?" Gabe said, following on my heels.

"Do you not know where we are?" I glared back at him.

"Sorry, Google Maps, my internal GPS must be on the fritz. I know we're somewhere near Emory University. Do I get points for that?" He grinned mischievously.

I rolled my eyes and waved a hand at the buildings in front of us. "Welcome to Yerkes National Primate Research Center."

"Primate Research Center? Like monkeys and stuff? They do testing on monkeys?" he questioned.

I nodded, and instead of going to the front doors I made my way around the side of the buildings.

I felt Gabe stop, so I did likewise. I turned and watched his eyes dart from me to the building and then back again.

"Aren't we going inside?" he said hesitantly, like he was afraid of my answer no matter what it might be.

"Nope." I shook my head and resumed my trek.

We had almost completed a full circle around the building before Gabe spoke again. "Are you going to tell me what you're up to, or do I have to keep guessing?"

I bit my lower lip and continued to scan the building. I was afraid to say it out loud; saying it out loud made everything a lot more real. Right now, I was just existing one step at a time. I still wasn't sure if I had the guts to go through with it all. There was so much that could go wrong, or I could chicken out. My resolve had been so much more certain when I sat safely at home in my bedroom. But now that I was here and it was all happening, it was hard to think about it all. There was still a chance I could abort this crazy scheme.

Then I pictured her sad, knowing eyes staring out from her lonely cage. How she would watch me whenever I was in the room and silently plead with me to help her. They called her EP13 or Experiment 13, but I called her Lucky when no one could hear me. My heart ached as I remembered how just yesterday Lucky reached her hand out to me and cried when I had to let go. I knew then that I couldn't just leave her in there. Thinking about her now caused my pace to quicken. I drew in a shaky breath and continued my search for security cameras, rounding the last corner that would bring us back to where we started. That was when someone tackled me from behind.

I swore quietly, just barely catching myself before face planting into the stringy Atlanta grass, still warm from the summer sun's heat. I was about to let loose a much louder verbal reprimand when Gabe's hand clamped over my mouth, and he shoved me lower to the ground. I followed his gaze and watched a campus patrol car glide slowly up the small road in front of us. The headlights coasted smoothly over the spot I had just vacated.

I could feel Gabe's breath behind my ear and fought the chill that snuck towards my spine. Neither of us dared to move as the car crept closer. We could hear the bass thumping before the cruiser drew close enough to see the vehicle's occupant. I stifled a nervous laugh when I finally caught sight of the driver. He looked a little older than me, early twenties perhaps. He was enthusiastically pounding his hands on the steering wheel in time to the music. He hardly gave the building a passing glance as he rolled by.

Gabe shifted slightly so he was no longer on top of me and pulled me to my feet once we were sure the security guard was out of sight. I dusted grass off my pants and glanced down at my watch, tilting it to catch the light from the closest street lamp. I clucked my tongue.

"Are you going to steal some monkeys?" Gabe blurted out, as though no longer able to hold the question in.

"I prefer the term 'liberate.'" I shrugged. "And not *monkeys*, just *one* monkey in particular."

Gabe's mouth fell open again. He blinked a few times, as if trying to remember how to speak.

I pulled him into a large group of bushes near the side door we'd passed earlier on our trek around Yerkes. I yanked him down to the ground next to me and kept my voice low as I waited and watched.

"They have almost two-thousand rhesus monkeys at this facility and more than five-hundred are infected with diseases, mostly the herpes B virus, which can kill them," I whispered. Seeing his eyes widen gave me a small rush of satisfaction. "It would be dangerous to release them. I may be livid about what they're doing here, but I certainly don't want to put innocent lives in danger."

"So you're going to just take one that doesn't have a disease? Why just one?" He frowned.

I sighed and leaned my head back against the building. I tried to rearrange my legs into a more comfortable position, but there just wasn't enough room between the bushes and the wall. "I thought if I volunteered to help at the facility—"

"You work here?" he nearly shouted.

My look was enough to shut him up. I continued a bit more forcefully. "I thought if I volunteered to help at the facility that I could keep an eye on the animals and make sure they weren't violating the Animal Welfare Act. I never knew how hard it would be to watch what they were doing to those poor animals."

I had to stop and swallow a few times. The painful lump in my throat was creeping higher and higher, strangling my words. I blinked rapidly to clear my vision before continuing.

"The babies are torn away from their mothers and kept all alone in small cages. They perform invasive procedures on them, sometimes killing them. Watching it all happen day after day, I have never felt so helpless."

Gabe's lips slowly twisted into a snarl. "Is it really that bad?"

I felt the tears coming and didn't bother to stop them. "One morning I came in and watched as they strapped a young male to the table. I knew then it wasn't going to be pretty. I was such a coward that I couldn't even bear to watch. His screams followed me down the hall to the bathroom. I threw up again when they told me later that he'd broken his back from contorting so hard against his restraints. They had to euthanize him just to put him out of his misery."

His hand over his mouth muffled curses as his own eyes began to water. "Can't you report them? Get them shut down?" His voice tremored like my hands had for the rest of that horrible day.

"What do you think I've *been* doing? They just pay their fines and keep going. I tried petitions and lobbying—nothing has worked. It's just so frustrating…." In my anger, I nearly stood to start pacing, catching myself just in time to hear a car door slam nearby.

Gabe's eyes darted toward the sound, and I lowered my voice until he had to lean in just to hear what I was saying.

"The janitors are here to clean the building," I whispered. "I'm going to sneak in while they have the doors unlocked."

We both stayed quiet and listened as two men chatted

and laughed their way up the sidewalk. The bushes were so thick we couldn't see them, but that also meant they couldn't see us. The clank of a bucket and the jingle of keys helped us track their progress. I waited a few moments after I heard the door squeak shut before I cautiously poked my head up from our hiding place.

Gabe followed me out of the bushes. "So why not take more than one? The ones that don't have diseases?"

I let me shoulders sag and my head fall to my chest. "What would I do with them once I got them out? One monkey is manageable. I can hide one, but hundreds?"

"Couldn't you find a sanctuary or somewhere that would take them?" he asked as we crept toward the door.

"They would be considered stolen. No sanctuary would take in stolen animals."

He sighed and rubbed a hand through his short, black hair.

I tipped my head to peak in the door; the coast was clear. I reached up to quietly slip the door open and then growled louder than I meant to. "It's locked. Those idiots locked it behind them!"

Gabe sucked in a breath. "Are you serious?" He swore and tugged on the door himself as if he didn't believe me. "So now what?"

"I'll have to think of something else."

He was silent for a moment; a look of contemplation froze his face. Then he spoke slowly, "You could leave a window unlocked the next time you volunteer."

"They have an alarm, and it's hooked up to all the windows. Trust me, I checked them all."

"Can you get the alarm code from someone?"

I made an effort to unclench my teeth. "I offered to open and close the facility for them, but they said one of the supervisors had to do it, something about safety protocols."

Muffled voices came from inside the building, and we dove back into the bushes in time to see a light come on just inside the door. Looking back, I noticed one of the janitors squinting out from behind the glass.

His voice fogged up the window as he spoke. "I'm telling ya, I heard something."

The response was too muffled to make out, but it made the man smile and turn away from the door.

Gabe leaned in next to my ear and whispered, "I could knock on the door and see if I can draw them outside, maybe say I'm having car trouble. Then you could try to sneak in while they're out here."

I rolled my eyes. "I don't think that will work."

"Well then I'm out of ideas," he replied in a huff.

He crawled out from behind the bushes and headed back toward where I assumed his car waited. I watched the door for a moment, then reluctantly followed him.

"I'm sorry. I know you were just trying to help," I said when I had caught up with him.

"Whatever," he grumbled.

"I'm serious. Thanks for trying to help me."

He didn't respond, but his shoulders lifted a little straighter as we walked in silence to my car.

"Where's *your* car?" I asked just before I climbed into my own.

"Around the corner." He pointed back down the way I'd entered.

"Need a lift?"

"No, that's all right. It's not far."

"Ok, well, I guess I'll see you later." I shrugged and dropped into the driver's seat.

Gabe opened his mouth like he was going to say something but then closed it. He just nodded and turned and walked away. He disappeared into the unlit section of road. I started my car and drove home with ideas for possible rescue attempts growing more and more ridiculous as I went. I fell asleep that night dreaming of helicopters and elaborate tunnels and leading armies of monkeys away to wage war on those who would mistreat them.

***

The next few weeks proved frustrating and difficult. My heart broke a little more each time I left the research facility without the alarm code or any idea of how to sneak Lucky out. I contemplated quitting, but it hurt worse thinking of leaving Lucky stuck there all alone. I settled into my agonizing routine, hope oozing out of my resolve like a car leaking oil.

Then he came. I knew something was different about him, though I couldn't quite put my finger on it. I had been around enough scientists to know what he was as soon as I saw him. But there was more to his story, and I tried to figure it out while my supervisor, Dr. Cultsburg, introduced us.

"This is Summer. She volunteers here three times a week.

She helps clean cages and other tasks here at Yerkes. Summer, this is Dr. Smith. The head of the department called personally to tell me Dr. Smith was coming, so I wanted to roll out the red carpet tour. He's a fellow researcher from, from... I'm sorry, doctor, I don't recall what facility you said you're from?"

Dr. Smith reached out his hand to me and gave a conspiratorial wink as we shook. "Nice to meet you, Summer. Thank you for your help. The cages look very clean."

I couldn't tell if he was being patronizing, or if I was missing something. I just nodded and tried to smile.

Dr. Cultsburg glanced down at his watch. "Dr. Smith, I wish I could tag along, but it seems I've run out of time." He looked at Dr. Smith apologetically. "Would it be all right if Summer finished your tour?"

"That would be wonderful." Dr. Smith's eyes glinted with something that I could have sworn was mischief.

"Excellent." Dr. Cultsburg clapped his hands once, too preoccupied to notice whatever was going on with our mysterious visitor.

Clueless Cultsburg was barely out of the room when Dr. Smith rounded on me. "This couldn't have worked out better," he said. Noticing my confusion, his smile broadened. "It seems my nephew didn't tell you that I would be coming today."

My frown deepened.

Dr. Smith chuckled and leaned in closer. "Or maybe he told you my *real* name? I suppose I should have warned him that I planned on using an alias."

I felt my mouth fall open and snapped it shut, then shook

my head as though that could clear away my bewilderment.

His eyebrow raised, and he tilted his head a moment before speaking again. "My real name is Sotirios, but my friends call me Ross. I'm Gabe's uncle. He did tell you about me, didn't he?"

I shook my head harder this time.

"Hmm, well he told me all about you and what you're doing here," Dr. Smith aka Ross informed me.

My cheeks grew hot and I took an involuntary step back. "You mean about how I volunteer here?"

Ross grinned knowingly. "I mean about *why* you volunteer here."

"I have no idea what you're talking about," I stammered unconvincingly.

He chuckled. "Don't worry, your secret is safe with me. I'm actually here to see if I can help you."

This time I didn't bother closing my mouth when it fell open.

Ross went on. "My name isn't really Dr. Smith, but I do have a PhD. I'm also really a researcher like Dr. Cultsburg, I just happen to be the kind that doesn't believe in doing harmful experiments on animals."

My heart surged in my chest as hope flooded back to my wounded soul.

"I think I may be able to help you free not just one monkey, but quite a few of them." He continued. "I don't have the means to transport the ones who are infected, but if you tell me which ones aren't, I can help you get them out of here and take them somewhere safe."

I sucked in a breath. "Somewhere safe? They'll be reported as missing, if they show up at an animal sanctuary they'll put two and two together and know they were taken from here."

Ross shrugged and checked over his shoulder to make sure we were still alone. "It just so happens I know a place that will take them, no questions asked. Somewhere they won't be found."

I narrowed my eyes and looked at him through my lashes. "Where, what place?"

His face grew serious. "It's the lab where I work. It's in a secret location with an animal sanctuary where we take other animals that have been… er, *removed* from testing facilities in a manner that might not be considered, um, above board exactly."

He noticed my skeptical look and added, "It may seem a little unbelievable, but it's true. Why else would I be here offering to help you if I was making up some super-secret haven for animals?"

I thought about it for a while but couldn't come up with a plausible answer. I chewed on a thumbnail as I tried to figure out the whole bizarre situation. In the end, it was his next statement that finally convinced me to give him the benefit of the doubt.

"Your only other option is to do nothing. You can leave all these poor creatures here, doomed to whatever fate these researchers decide for them." His soft brown eyes pierced through my uncertainty.

"Ok, so what do we do?"

Ross' eyes lit up above his pearly white smile. He rubbed his hands together and gleefully whispered, "I'm so glad you asked."

The rest of our "tour" consisted of me showing him which color cards indicated which monkeys were disease free. I showed him the exits, explained the alarm system and the limited closed circuit cameras, which were more for documenting research than catching criminal activity. I told him everything I could think of in regards to the schedules and habits of everyone who worked in the building. Finally I could put my time spent observing here to good use.

Dr. Cultsburg emerged from one of the labs just as we were finishing up. "Oh, oh my," he said, bleary eyed and somewhat disoriented. "You're still doing the tour, Summer?"

Ross stepped forward before I could answer. "I hope that's alright. I just had so many questions and Summer has been so patient and knowledgeable in answering them all."

This seemed to surprise Dr. Cultsburg. "Really? Well if you have any questions that our *volunteer* couldn't answer, I have some free time now. I would be happy to fill in all the blanks I'm certain Summer couldn't possibly have known the answers to."

I felt the heat rise to my cheeks.

"Actually, I think Summer *was* able to answer all my important questions, but maybe I could think of a few more trivial ones if you'd like to answer a few." Ross deadpanned.

Dr. Cultsburg blanched and then tried to compose himself. "Not at all. We are both busy men, I'm sure. I don't want to monopolize any more of your time. Here's my card, let me know if there is anything else you need. I'm going to go finish up some paperwork."

Ross smiled pleasantly and collected the card from a fuming Dr. Cultsburg. Cultsburg spun on his heel and stomped off towards his office.

"He's such a pompous tool." I muttered after he was out of earshot.

"But he has one thing going for him." Ross put a gentle hand on my shoulder. "He is preoccupied with his work. That makes things so much easier."

"Yes, I guess him being utterly clueless does have its advantages." I felt the corners of my mouth twitch up.

Ross suppressed a smile. "We'll take all the help we can get."

I sobered. "So what's the plan then?"

"I'll need some time to get a truck and some cages. I'll need to make some other travel arrangements as well. The sanctuary isn't close."

I bit my lip and waited for him to finish.

"And I'll have to find someone who can disable the alarm. But I think I know a guy. When did you say the cleaning people come?"

"Every Wednesday and Friday."

He stroked his chin in contemplation. "Ok, I think Sunday night would be the best time then. Fewer people on campus, no cleaning crew. We'll have more time to get in, get the animals, and get out."

My heart started to pound. "*This* Sunday?"

He nodded.

"As in four days from now Sunday?" My voice cracked.

"I think I'll have time to pull everything together by then. Let's plan on meeting just up the road on Sunday. There's that small carve-out in the trees, just around the bend in the road. Do you know what I'm talking about?"

"Yes, that's where I parked the night I tried to break in."

"Ok, get there and be ready to go by eleven… p.m.," he added unnecessarily.

"Should I bring anything?" I wiped my sweat-slicked hands on my jeans.

"Dark clothes, a ski mask if you've got one."

I watched his face to see if he was kidding.

He stared back at me with a straight face. "They know your face. Worst case scenario, if someone happens to see you they'll know who you are. But we'll all cover our faces just to be safe."

"What do you mean when you say *all*?"

"We need someone to help us bypass the alarm, and we'll need help carrying the primates out," he explained. "We need to be as fast as possible, the less time we spend here, the better."

I felt the unease building in my stomach. "How many people are you planning to bring?"

He scratched roughly at his thinning black hair. "That's the question isn't it? Enough to help us, but the more people you have, the more likely you are to be caught."

I sucked in a breath.

He noticed my worried glance and spoke with a calm,

authoritative voice. "Don't worry, I'll figure it out. This isn't my first rodeo."

I wasn't sure whether that made me feel better or worse.

"I'm off to make plans," he said as he took my hand in his. "A little fear is good, Summer. It keeps us on our toes. But don't let it overwhelm you."

I nodded slowly as he patted my hand.

He continued, "Just think about how in five days' time, many of these poor creatures will be free. And it's thanks to you."

"Thanks to me?"

"Believe it or not, I've had my eye on this place for a while now. But I needed someone on the inside who could give me the information that you've provided."

I felt goosebumps rise along my arms. "Really?"

"So when Gabe told me about you, I knew the fates had aligned and it was finally time to break these creatures out."

I couldn't help myself, I threw my arms around Ross and hugged him, hard. He patted my back awkwardly as I mumbled my thanks into his shoulder. I pulled away and dabbed at my watery eyes.

"Stay strong, Summer. I'll be in touch." He left before I could respond.

The next four days were both the slowest and the fastest days I had ever experienced in my life. I thought I was doing a good job of acting normal, but both of my parents kept asking me if everything was all right. Finally, I told them I thought I was coming down with something. They didn't hesitate to believe me; apparently I looked a lot worse than I thought. But that just made it all the easier to claim that I was going to bed early Sunday night. I told them I just needed to sleep, and they promised not to disturb me.

I felt a slight prick of guilt about lying, but the nearly overwhelming feeling of fear soon swallowed it whole. I quietly climbed the stairs to my room, inhaling and exhaling deeply in an attempt to slow my pulse and calm my nerves. Once the door locked behind me, I pulled clothes out of my dresser. I changed as quickly as I could with shaky hands. Finally, I dug to the bottom of my sock drawer and slowly removed the ski mask—the one I'd bought the same day as Ross' visit. With everything ready to go, I had nothing left to do but wait.

The clock stuttered towards eleven. I didn't know whether to wish time would go faster or slower and had mixed feelings when it came time to leave. I stuffed the mask in my back pocket, my car keys in my front pocket, and climbed out my bedroom window. Crossing the porch roof, I swung my legs over the edge and cautiously lowered myself to the porch railing. One last hop and I was on the ground. I moved quickly to my car, parked half a block up the street.

Just as I climbed into the driver seat, the passenger door opened and someone lowered themselves in next to me.

"Gabe!" I yelled. "What did I tell you about sneaking up on me?"

"I thought we could ride together," he answered with a sheepish smile.

"You aren't coming." It came out as more of a question though I meant it to be a statement.

"You think I'm going to miss this?" He was incredulous. "This never would have happened if I hadn't reached out to my uncle. You bet your sweet—"

"My sweet what?" I stared him down.

He mumbled something and focused on buckling his seatbelt.

"I don't think it's a good idea for you to go with us," I tried again.

He waved a hand towards the ignition. "Just start the car, you aren't talking me out of it.

I sat for a moment and studied him. I could tell by the thin set of his lips and the furrow of his brow that there was nothing I could say to change his mind. The car started without protest, and soon we were pulling into my previous, clandestine spot near the research facility.

"Should we put our masks on now?" I asked in a shaky voice.

"We should probably wait." He twisted his mask in his hands as he spoke. "If someone sees us walking up to the building in them, they'll know we're up to no good."

I bit my lip and sat for a moment longer before quietly opening my door. Gabe was at my side a few seconds later, and we crept towards our destination, keeping close to the trees lining our side of the small road. By unspoken agreement, we made straight for the bushes we hid in the last time. We didn't say anything for the first few moments.

When I couldn't stand the silence any longer, I turned to him. "Why are you here?"

His eyes widened in surprise. "Are you serious?"

I lowered my voice, suddenly fearful someone might overhear us, even though we hadn't seen any evidence that anyone was nearby. "This is serious. We could get arrested for this. So why are you risking jail time for animals you have shown zero interest in before now?"

"I care about animals. You think I like the idea of them being tortured in there?"

I didn't back down. "You've never come with me to collect signatures for my petitions. You've never wanted to speak to government officials with me. You haven't come to any of the community groups I belong to. So tell me, why now, all of a sudden, are you here acting like you're concerned for their welfare?"

He made a shushing motion with his finger and leaned in to whisper. "Keep your voice down; someone might hear you."

"Don't try to change the subject. Answer the question," I hissed.

I expected him to deflate then, to agree that I was right about how he didn't care and give some answer about how he was just here for the rush.

But instead he set his shoulders straighter, looked me right in the eye and responded. "I watched you try all those things, and I watched them fail. I felt your frustration each and every time you hit a wall. Talking and petitions didn't get you anywhere, and it killed me to watch."

I clenched my fists as I recalled all those moments. I felt a fresh wave of frustration wash over me.

"So I called my uncle. I'd heard stories about things he's done in the past and thought maybe he could help. We talked, and he got so excited when I told him about you. He'd been trying to find someone on the *inside* for a while. He explained what he was planning, and I knew it was finally something that could make a difference. I just had to be a part of it."

We were both silent for a moment after he finished telling his story. Then came the squeak of brakes. We look up in time to see a box truck backing up in front of the side door near where we hid. I noticed a dark figure hop down from the passenger side. There was a quick whistle, and Gabe stood up next to me and proceeded to dislodge himself from the bush.

"That's the signal," he whispered. "Come on."

I followed him towards the truck. The passenger was yanking up the roll door at the back of the truck. In the dim light, I could make out rows of animal crates, stacked floor to ceiling, filling most of the available space. There was enough room to walk between the rows, but that was it.

Ross came quickly from the driver's side and clapped a hand to his passenger's shoulder. "Ok, Mr. Black, you hit the lock."

Mr. Black removed a pouch from a large pocket in his cargo pants. He set to work, deftly hooking wires up to the alarm box near the door.

"Gabe, hop on up in the truck. We'll hand the primates up to you and you secure them in the cages." Ross tossed him a walkie-talkie. "We're on channel two. Just keep the volume low."

Gabe clipped the walkie to his pocket, then swung his legs up to the bed of the truck and pushed himself to his feet. He dusted his hands off and started puttering around the cages, opening latches and checking the straps holding the crates in place.

"Summer, I want you inside directing us on which animals are safe to take," Ross added.

I nodded. I walked over to where Mr. Black was finishing up his work. I shifted my weight back and forth until Mr. Black gave me an irritated look. I tried not to jump when I felt Ross' hand on my shoulder.

"Just relax," he whispered. "We'll get in and out. Just think of all the lives we're making better."

I took a deep breath, but before I could exhale, I heard a cough from somewhere near the front of the truck. I know Ross heard it too because his grip on my shoulder tightened. We both turned in the direction of the noise.

"It's probably just Mr. Green," Ross whispered without much conviction.

"Mr. Green?" I lifted an eyebrow at him.

He grinned, his grip loosened as another man rounded the truck and came into view. "Yeah, what's a secret mission without code names?" Ross chuckled and extended a hand to Mr. Green.

"Still not in yet, Mr. Black?" Mr. Green murmured good naturedly.

"Bite me." Mr. Black smirked.

"You're g'tting' slow in your old age." The newest arrival jabbed a finger in his friend's back.

"Mr. Green," Ross cut through their banter. "If you could head down to the end of the road." He pointed in the direction we had driven in from. "Keep an eye out for the campus security."

Mr. Green caught the walkie that Ross tossed in his direction. "Right-O, boss. I'll let you know if I see anyone headed your way." And he took off at a fast jog.

"Done!" Mr. Black stood in triumph. I noticed the red blinking light just inside the door was now a steady green.

Ross pushed a key into the door's lock, and with a click and a whoosh, the door was open. When he noticed my look of surprise he winked. "I may have borrowed this from Dr. Cultberg."

I led the way into the first room of cages. The night lights were bright enough to make our flashlights unnecessary. The primates started chittering as we entered the room, slowly at first as they woke from their slumber. I winced as the noise grew louder and louder. I tried to remind myself that the building was remote and the noise didn't really matter, but it still put me on edge.

I moved towards Lucky's cage, but Ross grabbed my arm.

"We start in the back and work our way forward. We do this nice and orderly, cage by cage so we don't miss any. Okay?"

I bit my lip, gave one final glance in Lucky's direction, and then turned to follow Ross to the second room of cages. We worked as quickly and quietly as we could while trying to transfer so many agitated monkeys. We settled into a rhythm, trying to spread our trips to the truck so we weren't all standing around waiting for Gabe to take possession of our latest refugee.

At one point, Mr. Black climbed up into the truck to help Gabe. Ross and I picked up our pace, and soon, most of the primates were loaded.

"We're almost done," Ross announced on our latest trip to the truck. "Just a few—"

He was cut off by a soft squawk of the walkie, and Mr. Green's disembodied voice floated out from the radios at both Ross' and Gabe's hips.

"Heads up, you've got company coming. Close up shop and get outta there!"

Mr. Black didn't hesitate. He secured his last charge in a crate and shoved Gabe out of the truck. He pulled the rolling door down as he jumped down himself. I stood frozen until Ross jostled me on his way to the truck's cab.

"Wait!" I nearly shouted. "We haven't got Lucky yet!"

Ross turned to me. "There isn't time. We can't risk all these guys for one monkey. I'm sorry, Summer. But we have to get this truck on the road, now."

"You go, but I'm not leaving without her!" I stated firmly.

"Summer," Gabe tried to argue, but I was already on my way back inside.

"We'll meet you at the rendezvous point," Ross called after me.

Yanking open the door, I heard the truck rumble to life, and I silently wished us all godspeed.

"Get her and let's go," Gabe whispered.

My heart jerked wildly. "Gabe, why are you here? You

should have left with your uncle."

"I'm not leaving you here by yourself."

I raced to Lucky's cage and flipped open the latch. The click and squeak were the most satisfying noises I'd ever heard. Lucky flew into my arms and we were frozen in a moment we had been dreaming of for so long. Gabe gently took my elbow and led us out of the building for the last time. I grabbed a soft-sided animal carrier on the way and somehow coaxed Lucky into it. The last thing I wanted was for her to run away in the midst of our rescue attempt.

No sooner had we slipped out the door, then Gabe was tugging me into what had become "our bush." Headlights swept over the bush, and I tried in vain to shush Lucky. My heart thudded in my chest as I watched the campus security car turn around in the parking lot, not far from where the truck had been parked moments before.

Gabe let out a breath once the security vehicle pulled back out of the parking lot. We waited until the taillights disappeared before we left the relative safety of our bush. Making our way to my car, I expected every little sound to be our doom. I handed my car keys to Gabe with a shaking, gloved hand. I knew I was in no condition to drive. I clutched Lucky's carrier to my chest as we drove slowly through the campus streets. I wasn't able to catch my breath until we were a few blocks from the University.

Gabe started to laugh, and I couldn't help but join him. I was in tears as all the nervous energy finally found its release. I let Lucky out of the bag so she could explore my car. I knew it wouldn't be easy to get her back in it, but I couldn't stand keeping her locked up another second. She hopped around the back seat chattering quietly, every few seconds coming back to sit in my lap before bounding off again to explore.

I had finally convinced myself that we were in the clear when I saw the twirl of red and blue lights reflected in the windows.

Gabe cursed under his breath and glanced at me with wide eyes. I felt the car decelerate as my pulse accelerated. Tears welled up in my eyes, and I spun in my seat to grab Lucky.

"Get her back in the bag. Maybe it's just a traffic stop," Gabe ordered.

"Why, did you blow a stop sign or something?" I tried to keep the panic out of my voice.

"No I...." His voice trailed off as the light circles came alongside us and then flew past.

I couldn't help it, I started giggling uncontrollably for the second time that night. Soon Gabe joined me with his infectious, throaty laugh. My tears fell as I gasped to refill my lungs. I cracked my window to let the fresh air in and the tension out. Gabe checked once more over his shoulder before pulling back onto the street.

It only took a couple minutes to reach the small parking lot that was our previously agreed to rendezvous point. The dirt on the ground was tightly packed from too many wheels traveling over it. The area was full of cars and campers. Locals had turned it into an impromptu used car lot. Gabe parked and flicked a switch, my headlights cut out. We sat in silence for the next few moments, scanning the lot and the surrounding streets for a familiar truck.

Each passing second built my unease. Gabe began to shift and fidget with increasing frequency.

"I wish we could call them." I had to break the silence before I lost my mind.

"Uncle Ross explained why we couldn't bring our phones. Nothing with a GPS. That's why we used the walkie-talkies."

I gave him a sidelong look. "I know. I just wish that right now we had phones so we could call and see what's taking them so long."

"I'm sure they'll be here any minute."

"You don't think…?"

"Think what?" His gaze was accusatory.

I held up my hands. "Hey, I'm sure your uncle is trustworthy, but Mr. Black and Mr. Green? We don't even know their real names. Maybe they decided to keep the primates for themselves."

"If my uncle trusts them, I trust them." Gabe's knuckles were turning white as he gripped the steering wheel.

I was about to respond when a pair of headlights flashed through the back window. We both turned in unison. Gabe noticed it first and grabbed my arm, pulling me down next to him until we were low in our seats.

"The lights are too low," he whispered. "That can't be the truck."

The same realization dawned on me, and I pushed myself even lower in my seat. I did my best to look out the side mirror, trying to catch a glimpse of the vehicle. I heard a door slamming and deep voices talking. Then the engine roared and the tires spit dirt and small rocks. I finally caught sight of the car as it pulled out of the parking area, the yellow and black made my heart lurch. *Why would a taxi be dropping someone off here at this time of night?*

A small scream bubbled up in my throat when there was a knock on Gabe's window. I spun my head just in time to see a man lean down to peer into the driver's side window. Just before my heart burst from my chest, my brain registered that it was Gabe's uncle. I placed both hands over my pounding heart and inhaled deeply four or five times before climbing out of the car after Gabe.

"…taxi, what happened?"

I missed the beginning of Gabe's sentence.

"Campus security was onto us. Somehow they noticed we didn't have the right vendor permit hanging from the rearview mirror. Of course we had to cross paths with the one rent-a-cop who thinks he's some super sleuth. We tried to shake him after we got off campus but he drove like a maniac, and we couldn't lose him. We had to ditch the truck and split up on foot in a residential neighborhood."

I lost all semblance of self-control. "Ditch the truck!"

Ross reached out a hand, but I pulled my shoulder away from his grasp.

"I'm so sorry, Summer. There was nothing else we could do."

I started pacing. All those poor animals would be returned to the horrors of the research facility or worse, they would be euthanized if the scientists thought they were no longer viable for testing. I doubled over and retched next to my car. A gentle hand reached down to pull my hair back and another hand began to rub my back slowly as I continued to lean over my knees. My empty stomach yielded nothing but painful gagging.

When I was finally able to stand, my watery gaze landed first on Gabe clenching and unclenching his fists. I wiped my mouth and turned to face Ross, knowing exactly what he'd say but still having to ask the question that was burning inside me.

"What now? Can we try again?"

Fresh tears fell as I watched Ross shake his head sadly.

"There'll be too much heat on the place now. I'm so, so sorry."

Gabe came and stood next to me. "What if we wait a while?"

"They are going to be even more on guard for a break-in in the future. I just don't think the risk will die down enough to get anyone to agree to help." Ross' dark eyes set into a hard expression.

"Mr. Green and Mr. Black?" I asked.

"I'm sure they got away, but there's no chance they'll help try again," Ross explained.

Then I remembered something. "What about Lucky?"

"I know you were especially attached to her but even getting just one monkey out would be next to impossible."

"What?" It took me a moment to understand what he was saying. "No, I mean what do we do with her? We were able to get her out. She's in the car."

Ross' eyes widened, and he threw himself against the car like a child looking into the window of a toy store. Lucky jumped around, screeching in the backseat, staring at us with wild eyes.

"Well one is better than none." Ross smiled, but it didn't reach his eyes. "We better get going. The longer we stand around out here the more suspicious we look."

I climbed into the back and Lucky jumped into my arms. She sat in my lap for the whole ride back to Gabe's house. She was quiet, but her eyes never stopped darting around. We sat in silence as Gabe ran inside to grab Ross' suitcase.

Once the suitcase was in the trunk and Gabe was once more behind the wheel, Ross finally broke the quiet. "There's a small farm south of here that has a private runway. I've got a plane waiting for me there."

He punched the address into his phone's GPS. We rode the whole way there just listening to the feminine voice telling us which way to turn.

The grass runway was at the end of a gravel road that wound through a grove of peach trees. I could smell the sweet, tangy scent of ripe peaches waft through the open window as we pulled through the darkened orchard. The headlamps cut through the dust and darkness and carved out a path to our destination. When we broke through the tree line, the runway stretched out before us. A quick look left and right and I finally spotted the plane sitting quietly at the far end of the open field.

We pulled to a slow stop near the plane and Gabe and Ross waited while I worked to get Lucky back into the travel carrier. I had a few scratches by the time I zipped her safely inside. We climbed out of the car, and I held the bag tightly in my fists.

I swallowed around the painful lump in my throat. "You will take her somewhere safe?"

Ross nodded. "Of course."

"Will I be able to come see her?"

Ross' hardened expression turn melancholy. "I'm afraid that won't be possible."

"Why not?" Gabe asked before I could.

"The sanctuary is somewhere… well, let's just say it's a very closely guarded secret."

As if reading my mind, Gabe spoke again. "How come you know about it then?"

The left corner of Ross' mouth quirked up. "I work there. It's a small community of scientists who believe that scientific discovery should be done to benefit *all* mankind. And we believe it should be done without harming animals."

"What if I want to work there?" I cut in.

Ross chuckled. "Tell you what, if you become a research scientist and you keep advocating for animals the way you do, and one day I'll nominate you for a position with us."

He noticed my confused look and explained. "That's the way we add new scientists to our team. Someone has to nominate them."

I bit my lip to hold back the tears as I whispered my goodbyes to Lucky. Gabe and Ross hugged, and I tried to shake Ross' hand but he pulled me into a hug as well. Gabe and I sat on the hood of my car while Ross' plane warmed up and taxied down the runway. And as we watched, I vowed to myself that I would see Lucky again one day.

Author Bio

Kara Piazza has always been a storyteller. For many years, she relied on verbal storytelling but decided to take it to another level with the written word. She is the author of *The Maladroit*, a suspenseful, funny, fast-paced tale about a woman and a quirky bulldog with a bit of science  fiction thrown in. She is currently working on the sequel to *The Maladroit* called *Nowhere Island* that will be published in the summer/fall of 2018. She also has a young adult sci-fi series planned and has the first two books finished, so be on the look out for *The Seeker Initiative*. She loves to help other authors and does so by offering lots of resources on her blog www.thewritingpiazza.com/blog/.

His Dog

by Frances Pauli

I pace the prison chamber, dreaming of the out of doors. My paws leave no impressions on the cold floor. No breeze in my fur, no scent inside white walls, and that lack of odor worms into my thoughts. Sterile—no cues and nothing to aide my judgment of the situation.

There is only the empty window, a sleek panel which shows more white beyond, more nothing. I curl on the metal bench and stare suspiciously at the hatch below it, at the button beside that. Their purpose vexes me as does my presence here where the air carries no smell.

I dream of grass, kicking my legs in my sleep and pretending I don't know it's a ruse. The world is no longer green. There are no squirrels in my cell. That part of my life has passed.

A man haunts the window. Eventually, I realize he is my enemy. I stop wagging, looking for friendship in a cold universe. He stares in with eyes that fail to register my plight. I need fresh air, need to know things still grow wild somewhere.

The button beside the hatch screams, flares red and angry. I cringe from it, pressing my belly to the tile and cowering for the man. *Help me. Make the sound stop.* My whimpering moves him only to frown. The red dies quickly, and the little hatch opens. Something falls into the room, carrying a faint scent.

Food, my nose insists, but this thing is dull and dry and too small to smell so good.

When I resist the bait, the button howls again. I've angered it. Perhaps, the smelly pebble is an offering. Perhaps, I've misjudged the man. I slink forward and the noise dies.

Relieved, I lip at the speck of food, find flavor wrapped around what might have been a rock. My tongue enjoys it, but the moment I swallow, dryness fills my throat.

Not exactly food, but at least I've assuaged the red button. In blissful silence, I pad to the water basin and drink the aftertaste away.

***

I learn quickly what the man wants. He's an easy creature, simple in his needs. Every time his face appears at the window, I pad to the hatch and wait. Resist wagging. It does no good anyway.

Despite the treats, I am certain he is not my friend.

When the light comes, I eat his morsel. The sound dies, and I am free to dream again. His game is odd but easy to endure. His treats are dry, but the water basin never stops flowing.

Today the buzzer doesn't come. The man watches me, staring with a new expression. No treat. No red flashing. I can feel his expectation through the glass. *What do you want from me?* Though he never asked for my friendship, my tail whisks against the tiles in apology.

Behind the window the man sags. Despite myself, I whine for him. I feel the inborn need of my kind to comfort, to befriend. Perhaps his device isn't working. I pad to the hatch, press my cool nose to the button, and then claw at my ears when the screeching begins. The light flashes. Behind the pain of it, I see the man's joy. I wag again, and my treat drops to the tiles.

We play it like this for days. I suspect it gives him satisfaction that I initiate my own torture. Still I push the button, eat the treat, drink the water. For three days more I dream of grass and wake to play the game again.

On the fourth day, more men stand outside my cell. My torturer smiles for them. When I press the button, they clap him on the back. Everyone is happy. Everyone outside my room, that is. His peers shout congratulations while I choke down my tasty rock and think.

What would happen if I didn't do it?

***

It takes a week for him to give up after I stop playing. Even before that, my bones show through my fur, and my steps drag against the tiles. The man outside the window wanes as I do. His face grows bristles, and he forgets to groom himself. We'll go down together in the end.

Perhaps they stopped feeding him too. Perhaps, outside my box there is another button, a hatch where his treats fall. Does someone punish him for my lack of cooperation? I consider moving to the button, enduring the torture for us both, but now my heart isn't in it. Not even to save him.

When the door opens, I cringe against the far wall. I forgot my prison has a door. I forgot the sound of his feet against the tiles. One of us whines when he clips on my collar, but we both drag down the long hallway. We are both weak and reluctant to move.

I almost remember my training when we reach the grass, but I fail once and try to stand upright. His barked command sends me to the ground again. I remember that we're supposed to cower, that they don't like it when we act too much like them.

It's a soft reprimand anyway. He has no more strength than me. Still, the grass is cool and velvety underneath my paws, and the air is full of scents. My poor nostrils ache. I devour my world with each breath, try to nurse the pain in my middle by eating the smells.

The man walks beside me, and I feel his steps stuttering. Mine are growing stronger, and by the time we sit beneath the tree he's chosen, I feel light, ready to eat again. I try to say it with a look. *I'll play the game. I'll push the button.* But oh, to breathe a little first, to feel the grass underneath us a little longer.

He pulls something from his coat. I catch the scent of food, but this thing is not a treat. It hangs heavy in his hand, cold and metal. I imagine a tasty pebble falling from the tube on the end, but the man lifts it to his head instead. He puts it down. He lifts the thing again, and I can smell his mood now, the pain of him, the scent of a cornered hare.

Or a dog in a box.

His despair moves me, but then that is my nature too. I whine and lean into his side, press my muzzle against his arm. He shakes once, and then he's weeping. His arm wraps around my body, and he sobs into my fur.

The power shifts between us. This I understand. He's been broken by whoever made him push his button, and I... I am stronger in the end. My tail wags through soft grass. My tongue bathes his chin, wipes the salt away. I am designed to forgive him.

The man drops his metal tube and then picks it up and tosses it away. He reaches into his pocket again. This time the scent is strong, the food he offers made of meat and juices. I eat a bite, trust him here in the trees and the grass. When he offers it again, I wait until he laughs and takes a morsel for himself. We share his food. His arm remains across my back.

Leaning on me now.

The breeze is clean and free. The sun is warm. I curl beside him on the grass, this fragile man who needs me. I follow him home. His dog, sleeping at his side with the window open.

Only dreaming of the red button when the wind is very dry.

Author Bio

Frances Pauli is a hybrid author of over twenty novels and numerous short stories. She favors speculative fiction, romance, and anthropomorphic fiction and is not a fan of genre boxes. Frances lives in Washington state with her family, four dogs, two cats, and a variety of tarantulas.

Too Close to the Sun

by Amy Fontaine

Dr. Kevin Forsyth was a brilliant man. A gifted neurosurgeon, plastic surgeon, and xenotransplantation expert, he had, over the course of two decades, played an essential role in everything from Botox injections and rhinoplasty to cleft palate surgeries, organ transplants, and stem cell research, quickly moving to the front lines of cutting-edge studies and saving countless human lives. He received generous funding from the National Institutes of Health and the National Science Foundation and was a health advisor to NASA when the organization was planning missions. He even won the Nobel Prize for his impactful discoveries in the field of regenerative medicine. So it may not come as a surprise that people forgave him for his eccentricity.

And what, you might ask, was the nature of Dr. Forsyth's eccentricity? Though he tried to keep it hidden from the public, the doctors and residents at the Forsyth Institute, his New Hampshire hospital and research facility, often whispered about it to each other while making rounds or sanitizing scalpels. When he wasn't assisting a patient, overseeing the work done in the laboratory, teaching a class, or attending a seminar via a video conference call, Dr. Forsyth could often be found wandering the long white halls, muttering to himself about someone named Daedalus. Sometimes, he was caught dozing in a pool of sunlight on the front steps of the hospital, with a pencil tucked behind his ear and a sketchbook opened to detailed images of angels on his lap.

At still other times, perhaps the most curious times of all,

Dr. Forsyth would get into heated arguments with visiting professors, researchers, and practitioners.

Once, for example, a resident, Becca Lebeau, overheard Dr. Berndreit of Hamburg chatting with Dr. Forsyth in his office.

"Dr. Forsyth," the German surgeon said, "the other day a man came to me and asked if I could make him over like a lizard, with a forked tongue, scales and all."

"A freethinker!" Dr. Forsyth said.

"A mentally unwell person," Dr. Berndreit countered. "Unbalanced and wildly delusional. I told him no, of course."

"How very conservative of you."

Becca had to press her ear to the door to hear Dr. Berndreit's next words.

"Dr. Forsyth, we all know about your cherished… fancies. As a colleague who holds great respect for you and your work, I must urge you to abandon your pursuit of them. Holding such foolish fantasies up as your highest ambitions will destroy your reputation. They are crazy and utterly immoral."

Dr. Forsyth laughed. "Immoral? They are anything but. We must accept visionary transformation as the newest and highest form of self-expression, the final frontier of human progress. It is not immoral, Dr. Berndreit. It is the future."

From the other side of the closed door to Dr. Forsyth's office, Becca heard a fist bang against a table. Dr. Berndreit's voice rose to a shout.

"It's completely unnatural, horrific nonsense!"

Dr. Forsyth shouted back.

"No! It is freedom! It is the elevation of consciousness! Mind controlling matter!"

"You're insane!" yelled Dr. Berndreit. "With your delusions of grandeur, your lust for beauty and power, your hunger to play God!"

"At least I'm reaching for something! I'm planning the future of the human race! You're just giving desperately unhappy people boob jobs and nose jobs all day!"

Becca heard Dr. Berndreit sputtering and seething with frustration in response. Then, to her great surprise, he laughed, and his voice became familiar and pleasant.

"Well, doesn't matter. It won't work anyway. Regardless, it was good to see you, old friend!"

"Likewise!" Dr. Forsyth said merrily.

Becca shuffled quickly down the hall before the door to Dr. Forsyth's office flew open and Dr. Berndreit strolled out of it, whistling a tune. Though he did not notice Becca as he walked past her, a flock of swallows swooping through the courtyard beyond the hospital windows caught his attention. For a moment, Dr. Berndreit stood stock still, watching the acrobatics of the birds with his brow furrowed. Then, shoving his hands in his pockets, he continued down the hall.

From whence came Dr. Forsyth's strange obsession? Rumors abounded. Some attributed it to past psychological trauma, others to his alleged experiences as a guinea pig in secret government experiments during the heyday of LSD. Others believed his passion stemmed from religious fanaticism. In any case, one day the Forsyth Institute announced out of the blue that it was closing its surgical hospital within the month and would no longer accept new patients. Three weeks later, the Institute's doors closed to the public. The windows were boarded up. Towering walls reinforced with heavy-duty electric fencing were built around the perimeter of the property. An endless stream of mysterious vans filled with mysterious crates containing mysterious supplies flowed in and out of the gate, which was manned by armed guards who watched the property day and night.

The doctors and residents from before continued to work at the Forsyth Institute, alongside a new, motley crew of top-notch researchers from all over the world. No one, not even their closest family and friends, knew what the Forsyth Institute's employees were doing there now. They were sworn to secrecy… and they kept it, in order to keep their jobs.

***

Despite the harried and frantic mood of his fellow postal workers in recent days, Mr. Lewis was in a cheerful mood on that fateful morning as he drove his mail truck up the rutted, icy road towards the Forsyth Institute. It was December 15, nearly Christmastime, and unlike many other mailmen, Mr. Lewis loved his job more than ever during this season. He loved seeing the New Hampshire countryside sparkle with snow. He loved wearing the holiday scarves his old ma (bless her soul!) knitted him years ago. But more than anything else, he loved feeling like he was doing something good and important every day by getting people's gifts and cards and letters, packaged with care and sealed with love, where they needed to go, to family and friends living miles and miles away. He felt like he was closing the distances between people with each successfully delivered present or message – thereby, in some small way, drawing mankind a little closer together.

However, Mr. Lewis's current assignment had nothing to do with Christmas. Instead of fruitcake, cards, or toys, he was carrying ten heavy boxes of research equipment of some kind to an "Institute", and the contents of the boxes had been classified as "SECRET". The descriptive materials for each of the boxes said only "For Icarus!" or "For Daedalus!" or other such obscure things. The equipment was under wraps because some kind of government agency was sponsoring it – the Department of Defense, Mr. Lewis believed – and, despite humming "Joy to the World" to himself as he drove, Mr. Lewis could not help but shiver as he approached the Forsyth Institute's gate and its armed guards, wondering whether the contents of the boxes would be used in direct opposition to the ideal of peace on Earth.

The guards scrutinized Mr. Lewis closely as his mail truck rolled up to the gate.

"What's your name?" said one of the guards after Mr. Lewis rolled down his window to speak to him.

"My name is Carnell Jay Lewis, sir," said Mr. Lewis, tipping his little blue hat.

The guard narrowed his eyes. "You don't look like you're from around here."

Mr. Lewis's warm, friendly smile shifted only slightly. "With all due respect, sir, I have lived in Grafton County all my life. I have worked as an employee for the United States Postal Service in Grafton County for the past fifteen years. I'm here with several classified packages for Dr. Kevin Forsyth. And for Icarus or Daedalus or Pegasus or... something."

The guard's eyes widened. He looked... scared? Then his poker face came back.

"We can take those right here," the guard said.

Mr. Lewis shook his head. "I'm sorry, sir, but I was instructed to deliver them to Dr. Forsyth directly. That condition is nonnegotiable."

` The guard sighed and tapped his foot. Then he grabbed a walkie-talkie from his belt. For about a minute, he spoke into the walkie-talkie while pacing in front of the gate. Despite the guard's lowered voice, Mr. Lewis caught bits and pieces of the frantic conversation.

"...Yes, a *postal worker*... No, I don't know how... Not usual, of course it isn't... Won't happen again..."

At last, the guard clipped the walkie-talkie back onto his belt and nodded to the other guard, who opened the gate.

"Come on in, Mr. Lewis," the guard said. "Go 'round the back to the loading dock. Dr. Forsyth will be with you shortly."

Mr. Lewis nodded. "Thank you, sir. Merry Christmas."

He felt the eyes of the guards – and the barrels of their rifles – follow him as he passed through the gate. He shuddered.

Mr. Lewis pulled around to the back of the building, to a cement platform that could only be the loading dock. Once there, he got out of the mail truck, treading carefully on the icy pavement, and stretched. Whistling, he waited for Dr. Forsyth with his gloved hands in his pockets.

Ten minutes passed. Then twenty. Mr. Lewis frowned as he checked his watch. He glanced toward his mail truck, with its precious cargo of undelivered packages. Looking around, he spied an open door on the other side of the loading dock. A strange blue light spilled out into the cold winter day. Though the light cast an eerie, painful glare on Mr. Lewis's glasses, he couldn't stop looking at it. Before he knew it, he was walking through the door. He shut it behind himself to keep out the cold.

He found himself in a long, narrow hallway. White floor, white walls, white ceiling. It seemed to stretch on and on into forever, with countless doors on either side. But the hallway was dark, except for the fuzzy blue light coming from behind a door to Mr. Lewis's right that was ever so slightly ajar. The end of the hallway was shrouded in shadows.

Suddenly, Mr. Lewis heard a soft whimper. It lasted less than a second, but the volumes of pain dripping from the small, sad sound tore at Mr. Lewis's heartstrings. Reaching out toward the door on his right, Mr. Lewis pushed it a little. Peeking into the room on the other side, he gasped.

A blue lamp shone upon a beagle shackled to an operating table. Repulsive gray lumps protruded from her shoulder blades. Her back was covered in bloody gashes and scabs. Her big amber eyes met Mr. Lewis's. Mr. Lewis's eyes watered.

Footsteps echoed down the hallway. Quickly, Mr. Lewis pulled the door back to its previous mostly-closed state and turned away. Mere seconds later, a man rounded the corner of the hallway, walking towards Mr. Lewis.

He was a tall man in a flowing white lab coat. Silhouetted against the faint light in the deep darkness, he looked like a ghostly apparition, an angel of death. As he reached Mr. Lewis and the pool of blue light, the man's glasses glinted as if they were on fire.

"Who are you?" said the man in a fierce whisper. "What the hell are you doing here?"

For a moment, Mr. Lewis trembled. He forced himself to stop.

"I beg your pardon, sir. Are you Dr. Kevin Forsyth?"

The man laughed. It was a cringe-worthy noise, edged with hysteria and pain.

"I am. Of course I am. The whole world knows it."

Surreptitiously, Dr. Forsyth reached behind him and closed the door that hid the blue light. The hallway fell into total darkness, aside from a tiny trickle of light from the crack under the door.

"Um, sorry about that," muttered Dr. Forsyth. "There's a switch here somewhere…"

Mr. Lewis heard Dr. Forsyth fumbling along the wall. Then there was a click, and the hallway blazed with brilliant, garish fluorescent light, the kind typical of hospitals. The blue light had disappeared.

Pushing his glasses up the bridge of his aquiline nose, Dr. Forsyth peered down at Mr. Lewis, frowning. Mr. Lewis smiled nervously.

"I'm... I'm Mr. Lewis, sir, of the United States Postal Service. Your guards said you would be expecting me. I was waiting for you outside at the loading dock, but... well, with all due respect, sir, you kept me waiting for almost half an hour, and I have a lot of packages left to deliver this morning, so I came looking for you. I didn't mean to be intrusive, and I'm very sorry if I interrupted you at your work."

Suddenly, as Dr. Forsyth examined Mr. Lewis in the light, he seemed to finally notice Mr. Lewis's blue uniform. The frown dissolved from the surgeon's face. He smiled winningly, dazzlingly, like the most popular teenager at a summer beach party.

"Ah, of course! Yes, they did tell me you were coming! I apologize for my rudeness! I guess the rumors are true; I'm as addled as they say!" Chuckling, Dr. Forsyth flung open the door to the loading dock, releasing a torrent of chill air into the hallway. He held the door open, beaming at Mr. Lewis.

"Let's get those packages over with, then, shall we?" said Dr. Forsyth.

"Thank you, sir," said Mr. Lewis. With one last glance at the door that was now to his left, he stepped back out onto the loading dock.

***

Officer Kim Luong, dressed in civilian clothes and flawless makeup, sat across the table from Mr. Lewis at the Starbucks in Hanover, sipping her black coffee. She had insisted upon having her coffee poured into her own stainless steel thermos, despite the protests of the barista. Mr. Lewis, however, had no problem with taking his peppermint mocha in the cheerful red disposable cup decorated with snowflakes, and seemed to be savoring his frothy, candy-sweet drink. Officer Luong rolled her eyes.

"So, Twinkle Boy, what exactly are you trying to get out of schmoozing me over coffee?"

Licking the whipped cream infused with chocolate syrup from his lips, Mr. Lewis smiled.

"I'm not trying to get out of my ticket, ma'am, if that's what you're thinking. I accept full responsibility for my carelessness. I will be happy to pay you the fee in accordance with city law."

Officer Luong sighed and waved a hand dismissively in the air.

"I already told you to forget about that. It was a minor infraction, and after your little heartwarming speech about seeing the twinkle in a child's eye on Christmas morning, you getting that package to its destination on time seemed more important than the fact that you parked in a No Parking zone for all of ten minutes."

Mr. Lewis wiped whipped cream off his nose with a napkin. Officer Luong cracked a smile that she quickly concealed. She looked out the window at the snowflakes drifting through the air.

"Well, if you insist… thank you, ma'am," said Mr. Lewis.

Officer Luong's brow furrowed. "Please don't call me ma'am. It makes me feel old."

Mr. Lewis's eyes widened. "Oh! I'm sorry, officer. I didn't mean it that way. You certainly don't look…"

Stumbling over his tongue, Mr. Lewis looked down at the table, clasping his trembling hands together.

Officer Luong kept staring out the window. It was December 18, and strands of tinsel wound around each of the lampposts on the street outside like fuzzy green and gold snakes. Looking out at the snowy street as well, Mr. Lewis shivered. Then he turned and looked intently at Officer Luong, a frown on his usually pleasant face.

"I want to report suspected animal abuse," Mr. Lewis said quietly.

Officer Luong's eyes widened. She lowered her thermos with shaking hands, leaning across the table towards Mr. Lewis.

"Animal abuse?" whispered Officer Luong.

Mr. Lewis looked steadily into Officer Luong's eyes. "I… I think so. I was delivering a package to someone, and I saw something… horrible." Mr. Lewis shuddered.

Officer Luong frowned. Impulsively, she reached for a stir stick, popped off the top of her thermos, and started swirling the stick around and around in her coffee, which had nothing in it worth stirring.

"Where was this, Mr. Lewis? What did you see? Do you have any evidence?"

Mr. Lewis sighed. "No, unfortunately I don't have evidence. I just caught a fleeting glimpse." Mr. Lewis tapped his fingers on the table nervously. "It was at the Forsyth Institute. There was a dog, and a man named Kevin Forsyth, and…"

Dropping the stir stick into her thermos, Officer Luong gasped. "You mean *the* Kevin Forsyth? The Nobel Prize-winning surgeon and world-renowned researcher at that facility outside of Lebanon?"

Mr. Lewis's brow furrowed. "Um, yeah, I guess that's him."

Officer Luong fished the stir stick from her coffee and placed it on a napkin. "I've heard other officers talking about that place for months now, ever since the hospital closed its doors. Questionable permits, mysterious shipments, experiments veiled in cultish secrecy. It does seem like something weird is going on up there."

Mr. Lewis drained the dregs of his cup. Then he leveled his gaze at Officer Luong. "Why hasn't anyone investigated?"

Officer Luong sipped her coffee. "Well, everyone has great respect for Dr. Forsyth. They figure whatever he's doing up there is for the good of humanity. Considering how much he has done for the most vulnerable people in our world… deformed children in undeveloped countries, disfigured veterans, victims of drunk driving… I can understand the hero worship. Plus this new project, whatever it is, has the federal government's stamp all over it, so even if those of us at the county level don't know everything that's going on, we have to trust something that has their seal of approval, their sponsorship."

Mr. Lewis pushed his empty cup aside.

"But you *don't* have to trust it," said Mr. Lewis. "Officer, I am a federal employee, and I am begging you, please do *something*. I don't know the context of what I saw, but I know it was bad. Really bad. A dog was hurt. She needs our help. And there may be many more."

Officer Luong sighed heavily, staring into the coffee in her thermos like a fortuneteller reading ominous tea leaves.

"Listen, Carnell, I'll let you in on a little secret. Before I moved here, I was an avant-garde animal activist. I went undercover in slaughterhouses and puppy mills. I exposed them and got the animals rescued and the people put in jail. Everything was fine for a while, but then…" Officer Luong's hands shook as they clenched her thermos.

"But then, someone finally came after me. He followed me with a gun. He threatened to hurt my family and friends if I didn't keep quiet. So… so I kept quiet. And I moved away."

Officer Luong gulped down the last of her coffee with a grimace, as if it was cough medicine, and slammed the thermos down on the table with a little more force than she had intended.

"I'm a meter maid these days, Mr. Lewis. I don't do shit like that anymore. It's heartbreaking, dangerous, frightening. And for every life you save, there are a hundred deaths." As Officer Luong looked at Mr. Lewis, her eyes shone with unshed tears. She blinked them away before they escaped, and her face hardened again.

"You can file a formal complaint at the police station. I'm

sure if you provide details about what you saw, an officer there will begin an investigation of your claim."

Officer Luong stood up. "Thanks for the coffee, Mr. Lewis." She started walking towards the door of the Starbucks, but a gentle hand tugged her jacket sleeve. Mr. Lewis whispered in her ear.

"Please, Officer Luong. There's no time for paperwork. It's almost Christmas, and the thought of that poor dog…" Mr. Lewis shuddered, then went on. "This situation needs to be resolved as soon as possible. And if anyone can do it, you can."

Officer Luong looked at Mr. Lewis. His eyes were big and pleading. Puppy dog eyes. She looked at the little reindeer silhouettes prancing across his scarf. She sighed.

"Okay," whispered Officer Luong. "Let's go somewhere private and make a plan."

***

Before driving away from the loading dock after delivering the mysterious packages to Dr. Forsyth, Mr. Lewis had seen a linen truck pull up to the dock and start unloading dollies full of sheets and surgical scrubs. The workers had wheeled the dollies to the door at the back of the loading dock, where workers from the Institute took over, wheeling them inside. Now, five days later, Officer Luong crouched amongst the sheets and scrubs in a dolly in the back of the same linen truck, trying not to breathe too hard or let her heart beat too fast.

Stay calm, Kim, she told herself. *Stay calm. Everything will be just fine.*

More frequently, she asked herself, *Kim, what the hell are you doing?*

She wasn't exactly sure, but it seemed by far to be the stupidest thing she had ever done.

The truck rumbled along for a while. Stopped. Rumbled along, and then stopped one last time. Officer Luong held her breath.

With a resounding thud, the back of the truck swung down and open, letting in a blast of cold air and whitish-gray winter sunlight. Officer Luong quieted her breathing and stilled her trembling body, listening as a worker wheeled all the other dollies away. At last, the worker came and rolled Officer Luong's dolly down a ramp onto the cement, across the loading dock and right to the back door of the Forsyth Institute. The dolly changed hands there, and an employee of the Institute wheeled the dolly right into the building.

Officer Luong's heart was in her throat. She could barely breathe. She just curled up amongst the scrubs and sheets as the dolly rolled down the hallway.

At last, the dolly entered a carpeted room and came to a stop. Officer Luong listened carefully to the conversation that ensued.

"Should we take care of these now?"

"Leave them, Becca. The custodian will get to it."

"Right. Right. Okay."

Officer Luong saw the lights turn off, heard the door shut. She lay there for a while in the dark, just listening. She heard no more sounds. The air was still. Quiet as a cat, she crawled off the dolly and got to her feet. Fumbling along the wall near the door, she found a light switch and turned it on, looking around.

She was in a large supply closet filled with all the linen dollies. Sheets lay folded in cubbies set into the wall, and scrubs hung from hangers all around.

Quickly, Officer Luong put a new set of scrubs on over her clothes and turned off the light. For a solid minute, she stood with her ear pressed against the door, listening for movements in the hallway outside. She opened the door a crack, wincing at the slight creak it made, and listened again. She heard one set of footfalls echoing across the polished floor. She listened to them fade into the distance. She waited. The footsteps did not come back. Taking a deep breath, she looked both ways around the edge of the door and then stepped into the hallway, shutting the door of the closet after herself.

Standing up straight, with as confident and natural of a bearing as she could muster, Officer Luong walked down the hallway.

For a few minutes, she simply walked around the facility, scoping out the lay of the land. She smiled at the doctors and surgeons she passed, but for the most part they didn't even see her; they were too busy bustling from place to place. The hallway to which the supply closet belonged was octagonal in shape, with eight long, straight hallways branching out from the octagon's points. The inner walls of the octagonal hallway were covered in huge windows facing a central courtyard with a single tree in the middle of it that was barren and covered with snow.

Each of the eight branching hallways had a sign next to it stating which "wing" of the facility it was. Officer Luong moved counterclockwise around the octagon, exploring each of the branching hallways.

The Daedalus Wing looked like a plastics factory. The rooms in this hallway were packed with white molds of various shapes and sizes that were fabricated in 3D printers at the backs of the rooms. In the Vulcan Wing, Officer Luong saw scientists injecting organic materials from countless Petri dishes and other containers into these molds and putting them into some kind of refrigerator. The Chimaera Wing was a flurry of activity, with people running gels through a machine in a dark room, investigating the contents of Petri dishes with microscopes and manipulating them with metal implements, hurrying carts stacked with vials from one room to another, and doing countless other things that Officer Luong observed but could not comprehend. The Ovid Wing seemed to just hold three offices: "Dr. Arrietta, Human Resources Coordinator", "Dr. Rockwell, Interdisciplinary Systems Manager", and "Dr. Forsyth, Principal Investigator". The Psyche Wing contained chalkboards diagramming neurons, MRI and EEG machines, and disembodied brains and spinal columns floating in strange solutions. The Apollo Wing included a few large conference rooms with white boards all along their walls.

In the Pegasus Wing, Officer Luong finally found the animals.

They lay crumpled and afraid in cramped cages stacked

halfway to the ceiling, covered in their own filth. Nude mice with paired wavy projections protruding from their backs, fleshy growths emerging from their own skin. Pigeons with stitches where their wings should have been, wallowing in pools of their own blood. None of them had food, water, or even bedding in their cages, and no one was looking after them. As she had been doing throughout her tour of the Institute, Officer Luong filmed all of the animals covertly with her cell phone, keeping a neutral expression on her face as she wandered through the rows and rows of cages.

When she reached the darkest corner of the room, Officer Luong heard a soft whimper. Turning, she saw a separate stack of cages containing nineteen beagles, all with bloody gashes on their backs. They stared listlessly through the bars at Officer Luong. One of the cages in the stack was empty.

As Officer Luong sucked in a deep breath, a suspicious voice said, "Hey, what are you doing here?"

Whirling around with her heart in her throat, Officer Luong beamed at the doctor approaching her.

"Oh, sorry. You startled me."

The doctor raised an eyebrow. "I thought you were out sick today."

Silently, Officer Luong thanked her lucky stars that she looked like someone she had never met.

"No, no, I'm in," said Officer Luong. "In and ready for action!"

The doctor's brow furrowed. "Well, you'd better get over to the Icarus Wing. Dr. Forsyth wants everyone on deck for the operation."

Officer Luong nodded. "On my way."

The doctor turned on his heel and left the room. Taking one last shot of the beagles, she held her hand against the bars of one of the cages and whispered, "Don't worry. I'll get you out of here." Then she hurried after the doctor.

The final wing of the octagon was the Icarus Wing. Before Officer Luong arrived, the hallway was already flooded with people. She pushed her way through the crowd, squeezing into the room to which they were all heading, the last room on the left at the end of the hall. She struggled to see what was happening through the bodies packed all around her.

In the center of the room, a blue lamp shone upon a beagle shacked to an operating table, with bloody gouges all over her back and two strange gray stumps protruding from between her shoulder blades. Officer Luong sucked in a breath. It was the beagle Mr. Lewis had seen, she was sure of it.

Beside the table stood Dr. Forsyth, beaming proudly. Behind him was a table of surgical equipment that Officer Luong couldn't see very well from her vantage point in the crowd. Officer Luong tried to take as much footage as she discreetly could despite her awkward position, hidden amongst the other people in the room.

"Welcome, all!" said Dr. Forsyth, gesturing grandly around the room. "The day we all have been waiting for has finally arrived. I cannot tell you all how proud I am. But this moment isn't just about me." Dr. Forsyth looked around and made eye contact with several people in the crowd. "Each and every one of you played an essential role in making this possible. Our incredible polymer scaffold engineers, headed by Dr. Santini." A round of applause. "Dr. Bankowski and his tireless team of geneticists." More applause. "Our hardworking partners in comparative anatomy, embryology, and neurology from the Visionary Medical Society." Applause. "Every single surgeon, resident, intern, and researcher who has devoted their life to our dream." Applause. "And of course, our wonderful patrons at the Coalition of East Coast Universities and the United States Department of Defense!" More applause. "Thank you all for your dedication to the Forsyth Institute's vision. Humanity's future is made by people like you."

A final, resounding roar of applause. Dr. Forsyth smiled like the sun and clapped his hands, continuing his speech as the applause died down.

"Some say that Icarus flew too close to the sun. I say he did not aim high enough. At the Forsyth Institute, we reach for the highest good we can conceive: to make angels out of men. Today, we are closer to that goal than ever before."

Suddenly, the room fell dead silent.

"Without further ado, let us begin."

Officer Luong's heart beat as rapidly as a hummingbird's wings. She caught only quick glimpses of the extensive procedure, but she recorded everything she could. The gleam of scalpels in the pale blue light. The surgeons bustling about the table, engrossed in their work. Ratty, feathered wings being sewn stitch by stitch onto the gray stumps between the beagle's shoulder blades.

And throughout it all, the beagle's screams.

***

After scoping out the building one more time (and seeing, to her immense relief, no security cameras anywhere), Officer Luong returned to the supply closet and hid there amongst the scrubs until long after darkness had fallen beyond the windows of the octagonal hallway. She had already figured out her ticket to escape, the custodian's pickup truck, which remained at the loading dock long after the medical staff went home, departing in the middle of the night. She would have to be at the loading dock by 9:45 pm in order to sneak onto the truck bed. It was 9:20 now and she needed to head over there. But she had a call to make first.

Fumbling with her phone because her hands would not stop trembling, she dialed a number and raised it to her ear, clasped in quivering fingers, still buried in a pile of scrubs.

"Animal Action Hotline, Cheryl speaking."

"Hi, Cheryl," breathed Officer Luong. "It's me. Did you get the files I sent?"

"Oh! Y…yes, I did. A team is on their way as we speak."

Officer Luong breathed a sigh of relief. "Great. I've got to get out of here before they come. I just… My career is at stake, if I'm caught up in all this again."

"I understand, Kim," said Cheryl. "But thank you for contacting us."

Officer Luong nodded. "Of course."

Hanging up, Officer Luong crept out of the supply closet and hurried down the dark hallway.

Right into Dr. Forsyth.

Dr. Forsyth smiled down at Officer Luong. "I've been watching you all day. I don't know who you are. But you are certainly not our intern, Ming."

Dr. Forsyth wrapped his arms tightly around Officer Luong. She struggled against his grip but could not break free. Shivering, she stared up at him like a rabbit in the coils of a snake. Grinning, Dr. Forsyth leaned closer.

"Isn't this place brilliant? A pinnacle of scientific achievement. My old colleagues thought I was mad." Dr. Forsyth barked a laugh. "But I am not mad." His warm breath tickled her ear. "I am a *dreamer*."

Dr. Forsyth's hands traced the contours of her back. She could not bring herself to stop them.

"Just imagine the possibilities," Dr. Forsyth breathed. "Cochlear implants to expand the range of human hearing. New rods in our eyes to make us see like eagles. Prehensile tails. Hyenid jaws, gorgeously strong. *Wings.* Supernatural beauty more bewitching than the finest painting, sculpted onto our own bodies."

Before she knew it, Dr. Forsyth's tongue was roving across the nape of her neck. She shuddered. Mustering all of her strength, she pushed him away, glaring at him.

"You're a monster!" she hissed. "I saw what you did to that poor little dog. To all those animals! The world thinks you're this great hero, but you're not. You're heartless!"

Dr. Forsyth closed his eyes. "I stopped caring what the world thinks long ago."

For a while, Officer Luong just stared at the strange man

in the white lab coat. He looked like a pale shadow in the darkness.

"Well, you've been found out," said Officer Luong finally. "Your Institute is done. It's over."

Dr. Forsyth looked at Officer Luong again. His glasses glinted in the moonlight.

"Is it?" he whispered.

Something in his voice made Officer Luong quiver. Before she knew it, he had her in his vice-like grip once more.

Squirming in his arms, Officer Luong glowered at Dr. Forsyth. "My activist friends will stop at nothing. They will kill your guards if they have to. They will burn this place to the ground."

Dr. Forsyth frowned. "For what? For a few mongrels, some vermin, and a flock of ratty birds?"

Dr. Forsyth looked deeply into Officer Luong's eyes. She couldn't look away. She couldn't even move. Behind his glasses, a manic light glowed in his eyes, hypnotizing her with its passion.

"I want to elevate the entire human race. You're a perfect specimen. You could help me." He sounded like a little boy: desperate, pleading. His fingers stroked her back again, sending shivers down her spine. His lips brushed against her ear. "What kind of wings would you like, my dear? White and downy? Black and leathery? I can give you wings. I can give you so much more."

Footsteps echoed down the hallway. Pulling away from Officer Luong, Dr. Forsyth stared out the window into the courtyard. "The swallows," he whispered, his voice choked with sadness. "The swallows went south for the winter."

Officer Luong followed his gaze. When she turned back, Dr. Forsyth was gone.

The footsteps came towards her. It was the custodian. He switched on a light. "What the devil is going on here?"

Officer Luong looked at the man. "Leave," she said. "If you care about your life, leave now. Tell the guards to leave, too. And if you care about all life on Earth, please, tell no one about my warning, or the fact that you saw me here. This is a matter of utmost importance."

The custodian stared at her. He watched her disappear down one of the hallways. He heard voices shouting and a clattering of cages near the loading dock.

A tongue of flame leaped into the night.

***

Mr. Lewis sat at his armchair by the fireplace, staring into the flames. "The Christmas Song" played cheerfully on the phonograph by his side. Stockings hung from the mantel, and the lights on the (fake, but nonetheless pleasant) tree glimmered cheerfully.

"Merry Christmas, Dad!"

Mr. Lewis blinked as his son Ashante shoved a package into his hands. He smiled and patted the boy on the head. "Thanks, little man!"

Mr. Lewis tore open the wrapping paper, beaming at the contents. "A scarf! Thanks, buddy!"

Ashante grinned. "I saved up for it! It looks like the ones

Grandma used to make!"

Mr. Lewis reached out and gave Ashante a hug. "It sure does! I love it!"

Ashante giggled happily. Mr. Lewis examined the scarf in the glow of the fire. It had little cats and dogs with Santa hats on it. One of the dogs was a beagle. Seeing it, Mr. Lewis's face fell.

Ashante climbed into Mr. Lewis's lap and nuzzled him. "Are you okay, Dad?"

Mr. Lewis's smile returned. "Yeah, of course I am! It's Christmas!"

Ashante wasn't old enough to notice the strain in his father's voice, but Mrs. Lewis was. Getting up from the couch, she walked over and put her hand on Mr. Lewis's shoulder. "What's wrong, honey?"

Mr. Lewis opened his mouth to answer, but then the doorbell rang. "I'll get it," said Mr. Lewis. He grabbed Mrs. Lewis's hand and kissed it. Then he put Ashante down, stood up from his chair, and went to the door. As he opened it, a soft whimper met his ears.

A beagle sat on the porch, looking up at Mr. Lewis with big brown eyes, a red ribbon tied around her bruised – but healing – wings.

Author Bio

Amy Fontaine has lived a pretty wild life—as both a wildlife biologist and a writer of wild speculative fiction and poetry. When she's not chasing creatures—real or imaginary—through the woods, she enjoys traveling, drawing, playing guitar, and dreaming about what the world could be. You can find her work at https://amyfontaine.wordpress.com.

Maggie's Promise

by Robin Praytor

The big room held cages stacked three-high along the length of one wall. Maggie's cage sat at floor level where the damp and cold seeped in. Sometimes Barffy peed on her from above. The man shoved her in, bumping the hurt leg. It ached worse than before. She whimpered, listless, licked at her bandage, then dropped her head to the cage floor, unable to hold it up. One long, brown ear flopped across her eyes.

"Did you see Tricks in there?" Barffy asked. "They took her yesterday, and never brought her back."

"No." Tricks was quartered in the cage at the top of their three-stack. "I'm a terrible friend," Maggie said, ashamed. "I didn't even notice Tricks was gone."

"Don't feel bad, Maggie. You've had a rough couple days. Things will get better."

"Sure." She knew he wanted to console her, but his words lacked conviction. "I'm going to sleep now."

"Feel better, hon."

Maggie awoke in the dark. No light shone through the high windows at the far end of the room. She listened to the familiar night sounds from the other cages: gentle snores, mewling whines and whimpers, a random yip—some from dreams, some with other origins. The pain in her leg had settled to a dull throb. *She'd* dreamed of the little girl again. She had black hair, and she wobbled when she walked. Maggie had jumped on her and knocked her down. The little girl laughed and laughed. Warmth filled Maggie's chest at the memory.

Sometime earlier they'd filled her food bowl. She lapped water from the tube, sniffed at the dry kibbles, and forced herself to eat a few bites. If she didn't eat, they'd place her in a tinier cage—one where she'd be unable to move—and then stick a needle in her. Some of the kibbles had spilled from the bowl. Maggie used her nose to spread them around so it'd look like she'd eaten more. After three attempts, she gave up. She managed to stand in the camped space, then turned slowly in a circle, and squatted to pee. The movement made her dizzy. Exhausted, she leaned against the front of the cage. The door sprang open. Maggie fell hard onto the laboratory floor.

Shaky, but up on all fours again, she took a tentative step forward. Her leg hurt, but the pain was bearable. "Barffy, Barffy, wake up."

One of the dogs down the line called to her. "Hey, what're you doing out? You're going to get in trouble."

"Hush up, you. It's none of your business." She tried to wake Barffy again. "Barffy? You up there?"

"Yeah, I'm here. You okay? Hey, you're out. Ho-ly cats!"

The stranger butted in once more. "I told her she's gonna get in trouble."

"Never you mind. I'm not talking to you," Maggie said. "My cage was unlatched, Barffs. I just fell out. I'm gonna look around." Several of the other dogs were awake now, watching her, and talking excitedly among themselves.

She walked gingerly along the short wall in front of the row of cages and around the end to the next aisle. It was lined with tables and chairs. A cold breeze wafted down the passage carrying a riot of scents. They supplanted the bitter odors of the lab, and her nose twitched in response. She limped in the direction of the new smells. As she neared the end of the aisle, she saw it. A door. A door propped open to the outside. The cigarette odor of the night lady who fed them and cleaned their cages, mixed with the new smells.

"Barffy, I see a way out." Maggie hunkered down. Excitement mingled with fear.

"Take it," Barffy replied, without hesitation. "Hurry, Maggie!"

"But, I can't leave *you* . . . and the others."

"Yes you *can*. You have to."

"No . . . I-I'm scared."

More voices joined with Barff's, urging her to go.

"Run as fast as you can."

"Hurry . . . *hurry*."

"You fool! Get outta here." That from Grumps, who'd been there the longest of them all.

Almost at the door now, the cigarette smell grew stronger. Maggie could hear voices.

She continued around the far end of the aisle, and returned to the row of cages. "I'll be back. I promise. Somehow I'll get you all out," she vowed.

"Don't worry about us, Maggie," Barffy said. "Good luck! We'll remember you."

Gathering her courage, she peered around the edge of the door. The night lady and a man stood close together in an alley, smoking and talking. Maggie stepped over the brick that held the door open, and inched along the side of the building in the opposite direction of the humans. The air felt damp, and water lapped somewhere ahead of her. She hugged tight to the structure, moving as quickly as she could on her disabled limb. Her tail curled under, between her back legs. Her body shook with cold and fear.

***

Gupta Jindal slammed on his breaks. The tires on the vintage, Dodge Coronet taxi squealed. He rolled down his window, and the smell of burned rubber filled the cab.

"What on Earth . . .?" Something had dashed in front of the car. A dog . . . or a cat? *Could be a raccoon, too,* Gupta thought. He got out and walked several paces in front of the taxi. If it *was* a raccoon, he didn't want to go near it. A wounded raccoon could be dangerous, and it might be rabid. He saw them a lot when he drove late night fares. Like most Maine cities, Raccoons were a nuisance in Lewiston.

Gupta took a few cautious steps closer, then bent down, joints popping, and looked under the vehicle. The streetlight didn't reach all the way, but he saw a flash of white. He moved closer. A low growl emanated from the darkness, followed by a series of yips and whines. *Aw, nooo. I hit a dog.* Sick at his stomach, he got a flashlight from the glove compartment. Braced against the front bumper, with his head almost touching the asphalt, he shone the light under the cab. A small brown and white beagle lay by the front passenger tire. There was no blood, but the pup was visibly shaking.

Kartik, the taxi's owner, and Gupta's second cousin by marriage, kept a spare windbreaker in the trunk for when he got rained on while helping with passengers' luggage. Gupta, a retired machinist, drove only one day a week to make a bit of spare money and give Kartik a day off.

Upon retrieving the jacket, he reached under and tossed it across the dog, speaking to it in a calming voice. "Hey, little buddy. I'm not going to hurt you . . . well, not any more than I already have." Another growl turned to a whine. Gupta reached out warily to pat the dog's head, and then scratched behind one ear. As gently as possible, he took hold of a front and back leg and pulled the animal toward him. The beagle yelped in pain.

"Okay, okay. Let's try something else." He needed a piece of wood or heavy cardboard to slip under the dog. He scanned the narrow street that ran next to the Cross Canal, from where the dog had come. Lewiston was a tidy town; he saw no debris close by. Bright car lights approached from behind the taxi, accompanied by the half-whoop of a police siren.

An officer stepped out of the vehicle. "Stay where you are, please. You need some help?"

"I think I hit a dog. It's hurt. I was just looking for something to slip underneath to pull it out." The policeman approached him. Gupta backed up a couple steps so the man could see him clearly in the headlights of the taxi. He pointed to where the dog was laying. The situation had suddenly become worse. He worried the policeman would ask for his ID and registration, and learn that he wasn't licensed to drive the cab. Both he and Kartik would be in trouble.

Evidently finding Gupta harmless, the officer bent down

to look under the car. "I don't have anything in the cruiser that will work."

"I thought I'd walk a ways to find something, but I don't want to leave my taxi."

"Not much traffic this late. Go ahead," the policeman said, "I'll set cones out."

"Thanks." Gupta walked along the canal and looked into the alleyway behind the first row of redbrick buildings. The structures consisted of old, abandoned textile mills and warehouses that were yet to be remodeled into high-end townhouses. He didn't see anything to serve his purpose. The second alley looked more promising. It ran behind a row of active businesses, and was sprinkled with commercial dumpsters. A loud screech issued when he raised the lid on the one closest. He shone the flashlight around the empty inside. The lid dropped with an echoing bang.

At the sound, the door next to the dumpster opened and a plump, grandmotherly woman, pulling a cheery, yellow sweater close about her, peeked out. "Who's there?" she asked, timidly. He could barely hear her above the ruckus from dogs barking and yipping behind her.

Gupta executed a shallow bow. "I'm sorry. I didn't know someone lived here. I was just taking a walk. I thought I heard a noise coming from the dumpster. Must of been your dogs." No need to go into a lot of detail about the accident, and based on the yapping, his circumstances would only distress her.

The woman pursed her lips. "A little late for a walk, isn't it?" She smiled nervously, and kept a cautious eye on him.

He could see she was prepared to shut the door if he took a step closer.

He thought quickly. "Sometimes I can't sleep, so I walk." He found it odd that a nani would be living in an industrial warehouse district. She should be ensconced in a comfy cottage, sitting next to a fireplace, drinking tea and eating fresh-baked cookies.

The woman appeared satisfied with his excuse, but still wary. Her eyes darted around the alleyway. "While you walk, could you keep an eye out for a little beagle? It got out earlier, and I'm afraid it might be lost." Her voice cracked.

The barking from inside the building grew in intensity; one of the dogs howled.

Gupta flinched, and his chest tightened—he'd hit *her* dog! He couldn't admit it. He and Kartik might be in enough trouble from the police. If she learned he was driving the taxi unlicensed when he hit her dog, would she sue them? Gupta had nothing of value to lose. But Kartik's taxi business supported a wife and three children. *He* could lose it all. "I'll do that. Say, what's your dog's name?"

Forehead wrinkled in worry or confusion, she stared hard at the side of the dumpster, as if the dog's name were written there. "Its name is . . . Buttons."

It? "Is Buttons a male or female?" After his wife passed, Gupta had felt as frail and alone as the woman looked now. And he thought she might be a little senile. Guilt weighed on him.

She didn't answer his question, but her shoulders slumped and she relaxed her grip on the door. "If you see my dog, please bring it back. I-I'll pay you five dollars," the woman said.

He nodded, and averted his eyes. He abhorred deception, but his obligation to Kartik and his family, prevented him from confessing.

She went back inside, pulling the heavy door closed.

Gupta spotted a flattened cardboard box wedged between the building and the next dumpster. He silently vowed that Buttons would receive whatever medical assistance it needed, and be returned to its owner.

***

On his radio when Gupta reappeared, the policemen called out, "I gotta go. I'll leave the cones. Drop them off at any substation first chance you get. And try the Lewiston Animal Shelter—sometimes there's a worker there at night." With that he was gone, siren blaring. The tension drained from Gupta. Relieved to have dodged one unpleasant, and probably costly, situation for him and his cousin, he bent once more to check on the beagle. It was still shivering despite the windbreaker.

Half kneeling, half laying, he gently maneuvered the cardboard under the dog until its weight was distributed evenly. Silent throughout the ordeal, it was difficult to know if the animal was hurting. It appeared lethargic. *Maybe it's in shock*, Gupta thought. "That's a good Buttons. Just a sec more." The dog seemed too far gone to respond to its name. With the cardboard in position, he slowly pulled the dog from under the taxi. The Coronet had a deep back seat, and the flat box with its cargo fit snugly in the space.

Gupta cranked up the heat and drove to the animal shelter, never topping twenty-five to avoid jarring his passenger. No sounds or movement came from the backseat. Every few seconds he checked on the dog in the rearview mirror, worried he might not find help in time.

Through the shelter's front window, only a nightlight shone behind the empty reception desk. There were no cars in the lot. He drove around to the back. A small scooter was parked next to the windowless back door. Gupta pulled up as close as he could, got out of the taxi, and knocked on the metal door three times, then listened. After repeating the sequence twice more, a woman spoke to him from inside.

"I'm sorry, the shelter's closed."

"I ran over a dog. It's hurt pretty bad."

"We don't have any drugs here," she said.

Gupta suddenly understood her dilemma. "No, no, I'm not after drugs. Really. I have an injured dog. It's in my taxi."

"I wish I could help, but I'm not allowed to open the door. If you don't leave, I'll have to call the police."

"It was a policeman who told me there might be someone here this time of night," Gupta said hopefully.

"I *just* can't. And I'm not a vet. Not for another year."

"But it's suffering. Is there anyone you can call?"

"No, there isn't. I'm a student worker. I only update computer records a couple hours a night. Please leave, I *can't* help you." She said the last in a stern, unyielding voice.

"Well, then . . . there's nothing else to do. I'm going to

leave the dog by your door and drive away. If you refuse to help it, you don't deserve to be an animal doctor." Gupta attempted to sound as stern and unyielding as she had.

As he removed the dog from the taxi, the woman continued to plead with him. He closed his ears and refused to respond to her entreaties. He set the cardboard with its bundle to the side of the door, and checked the jacket pockets to be sure there was nothing in them. For the first time, he noticed the dog had a bandaged front leg, and *it* was a *she*. Round, liquid brown eyes begged him not to leave. "It'll be okay, little lady," he whispered. "I promise I won't go far." He tucked the windbreaker tight about her. She didn't seem to be shivering quite as much as before.

When he got into the taxi, he slammed the door hard, started the engine, revving it once for emphasis, and drove to the front. With the headlights turned off, he slowed to a crawl, and drove to the back once more. He parked the car in a shadowed spot as far from the door as possible, but where he could still see it, turned the engine off, and waited.

***

Maggie snuggled under the cover the man had put around her. It smelled good, like the man. Spicy and sharp, but not the sharp smell of the lab; it was a nice sharp. It lingered on the back of her nose and tongue. She'd stopped shivering, but her leg ached. It'd been slammed hard against the street when she tumbled over and over in front of the big car. She wanted to lick it, but she was too weary to move. And she was *so* thirsty. How could she help Barffy and the others if she couldn't even move? She whined in pain and frustration.

The woman behind the door had stopped talking. After a few seconds, the door creaked open next to her. The woman bent down and pulled the cover back. Cold air washed over Maggie, and she began to shiver again.

***

In the taxi, Gupta smiled as the young girl, wearing a t-shirt with the letters UMA on the back, picked up the bundle and disappeared into the shelter. The sign by the front entrance said it opened at 11:00 a.m. on Sundays. He'd return the taxi to Kartik, go home for a few hours sleep, and come back in the afternoon to check on the dog.

***

Gupta approached the woman in the white lab coat who stood behind the counter, talking on a cell phone. He heard muted barking from the back of the facility. To give her privacy, he stood a few feet away and waited to speak until she was done. "Hello, I'm here to check on a little beagle I brought in last night."

"You're the one. Is she your dog?"

Taken aback by her abruptness, he eyed the badge on her coat. "My name's Gupta Jindal. And you are Deborah Birch, the veterinarian?"

The woman's attitude softened. "I'm sorry, Mr. Jindal. I didn't mean to be rude. Yes, I'm Debbie, one of the shelter vets. You're the taxi driver who dropped off the beagle last night?"

"I am. But, she's not my dog. She ran in front of the taxi, and I hit her."

"I just finished treating her. You didn't hit her too hard, because she's not injured. Not from being run over, anyway."

"She's gonna be okay?"

"I think so. I have some questions though. Would you like to come back and see her?"

"Yes, please," he said, and breathed a huge sigh of relief.

The barking grew louder as he followed the vet to the end of a long hallway and into a good-sized room stacked with cages—two cats in separate cages on one side and three caged dogs on the other. An exam table occupied the center, and a myriad of equipment cluttered the room.

"This is our recovery room," the vet said.

"Should I call you doctor?" Gupta asked.

"Just call me Debbie."

He spotted the beagle in one of the cages. She had an intravenous line attached to her back leg. He winced.

Noticing his reaction, Debbie explained. "She was severely dehydrated; that's what the line is for. And I'm administering an antibiotic, as well. She's a bit underweight. Do you mind telling me where you found her?"

"At Cross Canal and Evans Pine. Like I said, she just ran in front of the taxi. Must belong to somebody; her front leg was bandaged." He averted his eyes from the doctor to the beagle. She lifted her head at the sound of Gupta's voice. He could see she was feeling better already; more alert. Her tail slapped the cage floor twice and she lay back down.

Debbie nodded slowly and appraised Gupta. Finally, she said, "The dog's had surgery recently—as recently as yesterday. Unfortunately, the sutures broke and the wound opened. Something was grafted to her right radius. After x-rays and multiple tests, I found no reason for the graft to be there. I removed it. I'm not one-hundred percent certain, but it appears to be a synthetic bone material. The type used to build up the jaw for dental implants, for example, or similar uses—but to strengthen bones, anyway. I've never seen anything like it. It could be something new, but I don't think it was meant for animals. I have a friend who's an orthopedist. I've asked him to take a look."

Gupta was confused. "Was the dog's leg broken?"

She shook her head, and pressed her lips tight together in an angry line for a moment, then said, "I think she may have been in an experimental testing facility. And one that's unlicensed, or unscrupulous. Well, they're all unscrupulous as far as I'm concerned. The dog has a microchip belonging to a facility in New Hampshire. But I checked, and that place's been closed for three months. She also has a tattoo on her lower abdomen."

"So how did the dog get here?" Gupta asked.

"That's my question as well. The lab may have moved here. More likely, they went out of business and sold their animals."

Gupta thought of the old lady. "Could someone have adopted her?"

"No. She's had unnecessary surgery within the last twenty-four hours. That, with her general condition—my guess is she got away somehow. But she couldn't have traveled far, and I'm *damn* certain she's not going back. Would you be interested in adopting Maggie?"

"Maggie?"

"Her tattoo reads 'Maggie-5553927.' It's odd. These people don't care a lick about the animals. But Maggie's definitely her name."

At Debbie's pronouncement, Maggie raised her head and issued a short yip, her tail slapping the cage floor several times.

"See. *Good girl!* The number could be a product or procedure code—maybe even a phone number. Debbie addressed the dog, "You're feeling a lot better, aren't you, honey?" She looked back to Gupta. "So? Do you want a sweet, little beagle who would adore you?"

"Hmm." Gupta thought of the "sweet" little lady in the yellow sweater, and the dogs barking behind her. "Can I get back to you on that?"

"Sure, she's not going anywhere for a couple of days, anyway. And you should be aware she needs spaying."

"How much is this gonna cost?"

"It's on the county. Technically she's a stray. We usually wait seventy-two hours before calling a beagle rescue group … or putting the animal down. We still can—call a rescue group, that is."

"Can I put her on hold?" Gupta asked earnestly.

Debbie laughed. "We're not a department store, Mr. Jindal. But, yes, I'd be happy to hold her for you for two days, but not any longer."

Gupta inclined his head toward Maggie's cage. "May I?"

"Sure."

He lifted the cage door and slowly extended his hand to her. Maggie nuzzled the hand and licked it. Her tail wagged with more force.

He glanced back at the vet, who wore a smug, knowing look.

***

Gupta located the police substation closest to Cross Canal and Evans Pine, and carried the traffic cones up to the reception window.

"A policeman helped me last night, but had to respond to a call. He left these. Also, I need to report a possible crime."

The officer took the cones. "What type of crime?" he asked.

"I don't know what you'd call it. But I think there's an illegal animal testing lab in a warehouse next to the Cross Canal. I hit a dog—that's why the cop . . . er . . . policeman was helping. The vet at the animal shelter thought it might've escaped from a testing lab." Gupta didn't mention Kartik's taxi.

"What makes you think it's illegal?"

"Uh . . . I guess only from what the vet was saying."

"If the vet suspects something like that, I'm sure he'll report it."

"She. *Maybe*, I didn't think to ask. But I know where it is . . . or where it might be, that is . . . if it *is* a lab . . . ."

The officer was losing interest. He handed Gupta a clipboard with a pen dangling on a chain. "Fill this out."

There was no chair in the small space in front of the window. Gupta went back to his car. After entering his contact information, the date, time, and location of the incident, he skipped to the bottom where it asked for details. He reviewed the sequence of events. *At one-thirty, Sunday morning, I hit a dog.* There was a spot above for the description of a car. He'd leave that blank. *I met an old grandmother in an alley who had a lot of dogs and mentioned a lost beagle.* He imagined being questioned: "Why didn't you *tell* her you ran over her dog, Mr. Jindal?" *Because, I . . . .* He paused, unsure how to describe what'd happened without involving Kartik. Frustrated, he wadded up the incomplete report and returned to the station. The officer was on the phone. Gupta nodded toward him, and set the clipboard on the counter.

***

The next morning he returned to the shelter. It was better to tell Dr. Birch about the old lady, anyway. She'd know what to do. When he pulled into the lot, he spotted the same scooter that was parked behind the shelter when he'd dropped Maggie off.

The young girl at the reception desk wore colorful scrubs with cat and dog faces all over it. She smiled at Gupta. "Can I help you?"

"You're the lady that was working early Sunday morning, aren't you?"

"Yes." She stood and offered her hand. "I'm Lacey. And you're the taxi driver. I apologize for not opening the door, but—"

"Don't worry about it. You took her in. That's what counts. My name's Gupta Jindal. Is Dr. Birch here?"

"She is, but she's scheduled for back-to-back surgeries this morning. Do you want to see Maggie?"

"Not right now. Maybe you can give her a message for me."

"Maggie?" she asked, eyes twinkling.

Gupta laughed, "No, Dr. Birch... Debbie."

"Sure."

"Um . . . did the doctor tell you where she thinks Maggie came from?" he asked. Lacey nodded, and Gupta told her about the woman with all the dogs, who'd lost her beagle. "She said the pup's name was Buttons, but I knew something was fishy right from the start," Gupta lied.

"You have good instincts, Mr. Jindal."

"*Gupta*. Yes . . . well," he felt his neck and face reddening, and hurriedly continued, "I was hoping Debbie would go back there with me to investigate. The police might take a report more seriously if it came from her."

"Maybe so, but neither Maggie's chip nor her tattoo is traceable. And, if they *are* running an illegal facility, they won't let you in. I think the police might need something more solid than barking dogs to justify a search warrant."

"I hadn't thought of that. You're probably right," Gupta frowned in disappointment.

"Besides, Dr. Birch only volunteers here two days a month. She has her own practice, and she's pretty busy. I have another idea." Lacey picked up a cell phone from the desk. "A gal in one of my classes at UMA works with the local beagle rescue group. They'd jump at the chance to expose any animal testing lab, licensed or not."

The following afternoon Gupta met Lacey and five members of the rescue group at the intersection of Evans Pine and the Cross Canal. She introduced Marshall, the group's president and spokesperson, and Marshall introduced Gupta to the others. Each member wore a harness across their chest with a small, square camera.

Lacey had brought Maggie, who appeared to have made a miraculous recovery. "I thought she could help." The dog had clean white gauze wrapped around a front leg, and someone had added a smiley-face sticker.

When the little beagle saw Gupta, she barked, straining against her leash, tail wagging furiously. He bent down to greet her, and grimaced as she covered his face in wet, sloppy kisses. He stood, laughing, and wiped away the dog slobber. After introductions, he asked, "So, what's the plan?"

"Pretty simple," Lacey said. "We'll line up flush against the building, while you take Maggie and knock on the door."

Gupta shook his head. "What if they try to grab her?"

Marshall, the group's president, spoke up. "No worries, man. Not gonna happen."

Lacey continued. "They won't open the door until you tell them you found their dog. As soon as that door opens, we'll charge the place."

"Isn't that dangerous?" Gupta asked.

"Not the way we're gonna do it," Marshall said. "Lacey will hang back, and as soon as we're in, she'll call 911 and the Lewiston Sun Journal. Once inside we'll split up to search for the dogs, yelling all the while that the police are on their way."

"You'll be arrested . . . *I'll* be arrested," Gupta said, alarmed at the prospect … at *his* age!

Lacey patted his arm. "When all the commotion starts, you walk down the alley with Maggie. Get out of sight as quickly as you can. If we're arrested, they'll let us go later tonight or in the morning. The group has an attorney who works *pro bono*. Don't worry about us; the whole *point* is to make a scene and get arrested." She smiled at him reassuringly.

The machinist union had threatened to go on strike once. That was as close as Gupta had come to any demonstration or act of disobedience. He heard a whimper, and gazed down into the pleading brown pools that were Maggie's eyes. Gupta nodded. "Let's do it."

With everyone lined up against the wall, Gupta and Maggie took their position at the door. Maggie's head was low to the ground, and her tail hung limp. Gupta hesitated, then knocked on the door. The door opened a few inches. It was unlocked. *It's open,* he mouthed to the others. Marshall, who was first in line, edged forward, motioning the rest to stay put. Marshall took a quick look through the opening and shook his head. It was dark inside. Maggie whined and sniffed. Gupta pushed on the door and it opened halfway.

***

The door creaked. Barffy watched a shaft of daylight spread across the ceiling. It'd been two days since they were fed or their water bottles filled. Tricks never returned to her cage, and Grumps had left them in the night. No matter what came next, at least Maggie had made it out. His tail twitched, but a full wag took too much energy. He heard voices in the background. *New* voices!

It wasn't locked. Looks like they cleared out—there's paper and crap all over the floor.

Hey guys, over here.

Oh my God . . . they left the dogs to die!

Those bastards! If I ever get my hands—

Maggie's excited barking drowned out the rest. Somehow, Barffy found the energy to sit up. Maggie was right below him, barking furiously. She'd jumped up against her empty cage; a leash trailed behind her.

"I told you I'd be back, didn't I, huh? Just like I promised." Maggie's tail swished in a happy blur.

Barffy couldn't believe it. Maggie! Maggie had come back. The other dogs began to stir in their cages. People were opening the cage doors.

I count twenty-four . . . no twenty-five. I'm calling the shelter for help.

I'm calling the Sun Journal. If they cover the story, maybe we'll be able to find forever homes for them all.

At first Barffy flinched when a man opened his cage. The man smelled spicy and good. Barffy's empty stomach rumbled. The man stroked his head and scratched him gently behind his ears. Maggie was talking a mile-a-minute, but Barffy wasn't listening.

***

"Maggie," Gupta said, "I'd like you to meet my cousin, Kartik. These are his sons, Narain and Sach. And this little sweetie is his daughter, Fajal." The little black-haired girl took a few wobbly steps, then fell on her bottom next to Maggie. She laughed and laughed, and hugged the little beagle tight around the neck.

Author Bio

Robin Praytor spent her corporate days drafting legal documents and creating training materials. To distract from the deadlines and to-do lists that kept her awake at night, she invented complex and quirky stories that demanded written versions. Thus, her debut novel,  *Transmuted* (a KindleScout winner), finally saw daylight, and was shortly followed by *Mass Primary*, the second book in the Dark Landing science fiction series. She is currently writing the first book in a new dramedy series, *Evelyn Granger, Vampire Detective*. Each book will be a stand-alone mystery set at different points in history, or in the near- and far-future.

Presents from Earth

by Kara Race-Moore

The director slapped her hand down on the folder to get everyone's attention. All of the people crowded around the director's desk stared at her, worried. It was never good to be hauled into your manager's office for an emergency meeting, especially if you worked for the Mars Exploration and Colonization Company, but this meeting looked to be especially grim. A few people in the room looked like they were already mentally updating their resumes.

Director Emma Coggeshall, head of the Biological Experiments Department, looked around at the group with sunken eyes. "People," she growled with a voice that portrayed a night of no sleep, "we have a problem." She paused to pick up her coffee mug that read, *If you can't think like a rocket scientist, at least drink like one*. She stared at it mournfully, silently wishing the mug held something stronger than the swill from the battered departmental Keurig. "A weight problem," she pronounced gravely.

She took a long sip from her coffee mug as a storm of protests and groans broke out from the agitated group:

"What?"

"No!"

"I thought we finally settled this!"

"We spent ages working everyone's allotments out!"

"What can't we send on the supply ship *now*?"

The director put down her mug and waved a hand for silence. When the noise subsided she flipped open the folder and took out a glossy magazine, holding it up for everyone to see; it was the latest issue of *People*.

"I take it you've all seen this?" she asked, waving it

slightly. The cover had a close up photo of two toddlers playing with a space helmet like it was a toy ball. One toddler had milk white skin and bright red hair, the other very light brown skin and dark brown hair. Both children wore bright blue overalls. '*Kids' Life on Mars*' the cover title read, with the word Kids written in a crayon-like scrawl next to the block letters of the rest of the title.

"More fluff on the princess and little Bradbury," snorted Dr. Davis, the long suffering exo-micropaleontologist who was constantly running back and forth between the biology and geology departments.

"That nickname is getting out of hand," grumbled Dr. Sorokina, arms crossed over her UCLA sweatshirt. "She's an American citizen, same as her mother."

"But she's so cute!" exclaimed Sarah Palmer, one of the many computer techs. "Have you seen those pictures? Every inch a little princess!"

"It's sending the wrong message," said Dr. Burke, in charge of the botany group.

"Well, what *else* was the media going to call the first baby born on Mars?" snarked Noah Weiss, one of the department's interns.

"Better to be called 'Princess of Mars' than '*Pauper* of Mars', which is what she is if we were ever honest about the state of our finances," grumbled Shirley Cavalla, business manager for the department and account analyst for the Mission Experiments Subcommittee.

"Anyway," thundered the director, "yes, these day-in-the-life articles about the colonists do tend to be all fluff and no science – but it's the kind of fluff that gets the colony sponsors. And now, upon finding out that the first babies on Mars play with toys made out of spare parts from astronauts' tool kits, the hometown of one of the parents – Rodriguez's, I think – started putting together a care package, and it snowballed from there."

"Is it true that Rodriquez is pregnant again?" someone asked from the back of the room.

Director Coggeshall glared around at the whole group. "As has been said previously, the MECC neither confirms nor denies anything to do with the reproductive choices of the colonists." She glared around the room, daring anyone to leak something to press. "Moving on," she said in a voice as firm as granite, "the hometowns of all four parents – even Gregory's, because his parents aren't heartless, or at least don't want to look like it to the press – are sending stuff. And Hasbro wants to sponsor, as long as we promise to show pictures in the next article like this," she waved the magazine again, "of little Anne and Brad playing with the Hasbro toys that are now going to be sent on the next supply ship."

The whole room groaned.

"So, the good news is, more positive press for the colony, an uptick in interest, and Hasbro's going to give us money as well as toys since it's hard to buy oxygen and fuel with Monopoly money – even if it is the Mars' edition."

Her attempt at a joke didn't get a response, instead someone demanded, "So how bad, exactly, is the bad news?"

"Weight allowances are going to be cut across the board. Everyone's going to have to give up part of their planned allotments. Put your thinking caps on, people, and start deciding what you can do without."

Her assistant began passing around print outs.

"These are your new allotments. This is non-negotiable. I've already sweated blood over getting enough space for our department. There was an all-night emergency session with all department heads. You're going to need to submit your revised lists of what you're sending ASAP so I can get them to the cargo master for the new manifest."

"Look at this," one of the botanists exclaimed, pointing at the new quotasallotments. "Look how much space these other groups get to keep! It should be equal, across-the-board cuts!"

"Well, we can't exactly ask the crew and passengers to hack off a few limbs to decrease their weight. The Patel's have already agreed to cut their personal cargo in half – and you know how little space the colonists get to begin with!"

"Whose brilliant idea was it to give that interview anyway?" snarled the neurobiologist Dr. Nguyen. "Let me guess, Dr. Kennedy?"

"I think Dr. Kennedy was hoping something like this would happen," admitted the director with a sigh.

"Doctor," sneered Dr. Nguyen. "That Kennedy woman got her doctorate in *public relations.*"

"And her skill in that field has kept the lights on for the rest of us, here and on Mars. Remember, 'after the first hundred firsts no one will care anymore.'"

"But they do care!"

"Because of Kennedy's PR stunts like this one," said the

director, tapping the magazine cover. "So, back to work people."

Most of the group began to get up, grumbling and heading towards the door, but Dr. Nguyen refused to go quietly. "This is too important to be swept aside for a few pieces of cheap plastic!"

"Sorry, that's the way the cookie crumbles, doc."

"We had an agreement! I was given clearance for this project with a weight allotment of two hundred pounds!"

"You now have twenty. Good luck."

"There's no such thing as a twenty pound, adult chimpanzee!"

"Then use something else!" barked Dr. Coggeshall. "It was assumed when you were hired that you had a working brain! Now go use it!"

Dr. Nguyen stalked from the room and let the door slam behind him.

Back in his closet of a lab Dr. Nguyen grabbed a notebook and began scribbling a list of potential test subjects. He had already successfully sent several smaller mammals of the rodent variety to Mars in cryostasis. There was no point in replicating the success if he wanted his overall project to move forward.

He wrote down every mammal he could think of that was smaller than a chimpanzee but bigger than a rat. He crossed out most of what he had written, then wrote down a few more ideas. He paused to chew on the end of his pen, furious his experiment was being upended at this late stage. He wanted to prove large mammals could withstand the cryostasis process. Doing so would bring the process one step forward, perhaps even one giant leap forwards, to human trials.

Human cryostasis was the key to human exploration and eventual colonization outside of this little pond of a solar system—the way for humans to start getting out there to the great ocean of stars just waiting to be explored. Also, if he, Dr. Nguyen, was the one to figure out the process, it meant a Nobel for sure, and tenure at the university of his choice.

With a growl of frustration, he crossed out everything in the rodent family.

A small dog perhaps? But the types of breeds less than 20 pounds tended to be inbreed, with a host of health issues. He needed a healthy specimen. So, it would have to be a cat. *Hmm, no cats currently in the labs, at least, not ones that weren't already being used in other experiments.*

A few minutes on the internet and then he was in the car, headed for the closest animal rescue.

"I would like to adopt a cat."

"Wonderful!" The woman at the front desk had a name tag pinned to her shirt that said,"Vicki, volunteer." "Are you looking to adopt a kitten or an adult cat today?" she asked, cheerful as a kindergarten teacher.

"A full-grown adult cat please. Healthy," he stressed, "disease and parasite free, with all limbs and appendages, and in a normal weight range, no more than ten pounds."

"Ohhhkay," she said slowly, put off by his tense manner. "Any particular breed?"

"No inbreeding – a healthy breed or mix would be best."

"Hmmm…" she typed on the computer, then rapidly clicked through a few options before swinging the computer screen around to show him a display of several pictures. "For what you're looking for, how about one of these little guys?"

He looked at the different options and pointed at a cat with short, reddish-brown fur and large ears. It was looking at the camera with large, upward-tilted eyes, as if startled that someone wanted its picture.

"That one? Yeah, he's a sweet guy, but pretty shy, which is typical for Abyssinians."

"Healthy?"

"Oh yes. He was a rescue from a hoarder situation – I think it was on the news? That old lady with the uh, stuff, in the jars? But when he and the others were brought in we had them all cleaned, given shots, spayed or neutered, the whole deal. And he's one of the healthiest we got from there, which makes us think he was a recent acquisition. So yeah, a typical, healthy male cat. Shall we go meet him?"

Less than half an hour later Dr. Nguyen was back in the car with the cage, on the passenger seat next to him, filled with one rather confused cat. The cat made a low growling noise of distaste, most likely upset at the smell of the disinfectant Dr. Nguyen used to wipe out the carrier. Though arguably, the cat would have been more upset by the smells and liquids left behind by the carrier's previous occupant.

On the highway, Dr. Nguyen scowled at a billboard for L.L. Bean, showing two pictures side by side; one, a typical scene of campers outdoors, the other of the colonists on Mars at Base Camp 3. *Good enough for Mars – good enough for your backyard*, read the tag line.

Sending those specially designed exploration tents two supply ships ago had taken up space his group also could have used. Another growl came from the cage, as if in agreement with his annoyance at the sponsors' first dibs on cargo room.

Pulling into the university parking lot, Dr. Nguyen found a spot near his building, which was a miracle into itself. He pulled the carrier out and carried box and occupant across the freshly mown lawn. As he walked he took a deep breath, reassuring himself that all was not lost with the last minute switch in subject. He could work with this.

Back in the lab Dr. Nguyen set the carrier down and cheerfully told the new subject, "Let's get you measured for your cryo-capsule."

The cat hissed in response.

"After you've been sedated," he amended hastily.

The cat began trying to scratch at the cage door with its sharp little claws.

"*Heavily* sedated."

Once he had the measurements for the dimensions of the new capsule, he beganassembling the parts he had only recently put away after finishing the original capsule meant for a chimpanzee.

With a sigh, he cracked open a can of Red Bull. He took a long swig, then traded the energy drink for a Phillips head screwdriver.

"For Science," he intoned solemnly, and began retro-engineering a smaller, lighter capsule by dismantling the old one.

Two days later his lab was scattered with empty cans, brown ringed coffee cups, and slightly smelly take out cartons, as well as a newly completed cryo-sleep capsule, ready for its feline occupant. He, along with the others, submitted new weight lists, and, after a few more adjustments, the unhappy compromise was reached on what would go on the cargo manifest.

The supply ship took off on schedule, packed to the gills with cargo, including some of the newest of Hasbro's toys, including a prototype Princess of Mars ™ costume that would be in stores around the same time the supply ship got to Mars. There were also much needed new air filtration parts, and slabs of chocolate and tubes of toothpaste, and a crate of stage make-up for Dr. Kennedy's PR Department. There were sacks of flour, rice, and beans, tubs of coconut butter, and vats of olive oil. There was a cask of Madeira sent from Portugal to Dr. Vieira - somehow getting in under a religious category, and brandy and vodka that Dr. Mikhaylova justified as 'medicinal' along with the syringes and bandages and tetanus shots and penicillin and aspirin being sent.

There were jars of honey and cans of fish and boxes of powdered milk and dried fruit, and old fashioned letters from home. Also, bags of fertilizer and flats of industrial construction tools and boxes of replacement parts for the rovers, and new sunglasses and laundry detergent, and more.

There were coffee beans and cocoa powder and tea leaves which all had to be inspected due to an unsubstantiated rumor that had gone around a few years ago that marijuana had been smuggled up one trip in a tin of tea. The allegation had never been proven, but cursory inspections had been installed to appease a pearl-clutching public.

And nestled amongst all the boxes, bags, crates and drums, a little stainless-steel coffin whirred softly, carrying the almost-dead subject to Mars.

Almost six months later the ship landed on Mars, where the crew and passengers were more than ready to help unload the cargo onto the rover and get off the ship.

The colonist driving the rover, Alexis McGowan, shucked out of her blue exo-suit with the skill of much practice. She pulled off her long sleeved thermal shirt as well, the shirt being a necessity outside on the cold surface, but a sweaty nuisance inside the colony, kept warm with the humming greenhouse lights, the whirring oxygen machines, and the natural body heat of the colonists gathered together. Stripping down to her tank top revealed the sleeve of tattoos up and down each arm, a mix of scientific and science fiction symbols, ending with a cuff of lettering on each wrist, ironically quite often mistaken for Hebrew, but was in fact a string of Aurebesh letters that translated to: *What Would Luke Skywalker Do?*

She grinned at the rest, "We got freshies!"

Everyone formed a sort of assembly line and they had the supplies in the colony before the Patel's had finished the ponderous process of climbing out of the bulky blue exo-suits.

"I swear we learned how to do this back on the Utah base, and we've been practicing the whole way out here," muttered Pratibha Patel as she struggled to get her legs out of the suit.

"You'll get it," reassured McGowan. "Martian gravity takes some getting used to."

"It always takes me a few days to adjust," assured Zhang, one of the shuttle pilots.

"I thought you were an old hand at this by now," smirked Dr. Li Yunhe.

Zhang grinned and responded with something flirtatious in Mandarin.

"I bet you say that to all the Martian girls," Dr. Li grinned back at him.

Everyone gathered in the common area, speaking over each other with excitement at the break to the usual routine. Dr. Harper Kennedy and a _very_ pregnant Dr. Ysabel Rodriguez lead out the preschoolers Anne and Brad to join in the throng. The first girl and first boy born on Mars looked confused by all the commotion.

Commander Stang waved his hand for quiet. "I would like to officially introduce everyone to our newest colonists: Dr. Pratibha Patel, renowned astrogeologist, and Dr. Devansh Patel, award winning engineer, both of whom we are going to welcome, and of course, put right to work!"

Everyone in the room cheered and laughed. Devansh Petal couldn't stop grinning while Sabhitta Patel looked around like she was trying to take in everything at once.

Next, Dr. Kennedy coordinated a photo shoot and had

pictures taken of the new colonists with the six remaining 'Original Seven', as the media had nicknamed the first humans on Mars.

After that Davensh Patel practically fell over himself to shake Dr. Fitzsimmons hand.

"FirstStep - I mean - Dr. Fitzsimmons, it is such an honor to finally meet you in person, I had your poster in my dorm room in college, it is so amazing, standing here, talking with the first human to set foot on Mars," he babbled.

"All I did was open a door," smiled FirstStep, "I'm just glad people like you followed."

Meanwhile, Sabhitta Patel had already cornered Dr. Li and was asking, "What has the preliminary findings shown for the sample you mentioned in that report on last week? I have some new ideas for conducting analysis – I stand by my thesis that the voyage to Earth and the exposure on Earth's surface, no how carefully contained, absolutely ruins the findings."

"I have the samples and site notes ready for you," said Dr. Li, smiling at the other woman's enthusiasm, knowing the Selection Committee had picked someone else with the right level of dedication to make a good Mars colonist.

"Rest easy, Doctor," added FirstStep. "Stretch your legs, get used to the new gravity and give yourself time to adjust. The rocks have been here fifty million years; they'll wait a few days. After all – you've got the rest of your life to study them."

Dr. Patel's face lit up at that, the realization that the dream had come true, that she would spend the rest of her life making scientific explorations on the surface of another planet, making history.

"So, what's the latest gossip back on Earth?" Dr. Chadha asked the supply ship crew as people sorted through the boxes, making different piles that would go to the labs, kitchen, greenhouse, garage, and residencies.

Several crew members' eyes flicked involuntarily towards Dr. Kennedy.

"Oh what has that-" Dr. Kennedy visibly chocked back whatever she had been about to call her ex-husband and instead smiled and, with poisonous sweetness, asked, "How is dear Gregory?"

"He's been making noises about how his daughter should be raised on Earth," one of the pilots admitted reluctantly.

Dr. Kennedy snorted. "He can make all the noise he likes. My daughter stays with me and I am staying on Mars."

FirstStep put a hand on her shoulder and said, "Of course, of course, I'm sure no one else is saying otherwise. It sounds like Gregory's just... being Gregory."

Dr. Anita Sakai, on her way out with a tray of seedlings that needed to be taken directly to their new home, rolled her eyes while Dr. Katenka Mikhaylova muttered something under her breath in Russian about soured love affairs.

At that point Anne ran up to Pratibha Patel, hugged her legs, and threw back her head to chirp up at her, "Hi! You want to play Candyland?"

Dr. Patel froze, surprised by the enthusiastic greeting.

Dr. Kennedy pulled at her daughter's arm, "Anne,

honey-bear, don't paw at the Earth renowned scientist. Dr. Patel had a long voyage and needs to rest." She looked up, "Sorry, Anne tends to treat everyone as potential playmates. She doesn't know what strangers are."

"Ah, and why should she?" asked FirstStep, picking up Anne and swinging her up and down in the air, causing her to shrill with delighted laughter. "Her Little Majesty sees all us Martians as her loyal subjects, don't you?"

Anne Kennedy, first human born on another planet, continued to laugh at the delightful game of being swung through the air.

"Now, let's see what our dear new sponsor has sent, shall we?" he asked, moving towards the large crate stamped with the company's logo. Dr. Kennedy hurried to set up a camera to film the unveiling, fingers crossed the children would be marketably delighted with the sponsor's 'gifts'.

"OK boys," McGowan said to Linas Kalnietis and Dr. Joseph Harrington-Murphy, "we've got some other stuff that needs to uncrated now too. I bet Dr. Sakai's already in the lab and chomping at the bit." They all hefted up a box each while the rest of the group chatted and watched Anne and Brad play with their new toys.

Dr. Rodriquez pulled the Princess of Mars costume out and held it out by two fingers.

"Pretty!" said Anne, reaching for it.

"Yes!" agreed Dr. Rodriquez brightly, then whispered to Dr. Kennedy, "It's like the Borg Queen designed a coronation dress for the Queen of Hearts."

Dr. Kennedy grinned and said between her teeth,

"Hasbro wants to cash in on Anne's nickname and has agreed to a nice fat fee for the privilege."

"For the good of the colony," agreed Dr. Rodriquez, then groaned, "And I think my feet are swelling up again, I have to sit down."

"I can't believe you went back for round two," said Dr. Kennedy, shaking her head in disbelief.

Dr. Rodriguez placed her hands on her expanding midsection and grinned. "I told Donald when we got married that I wanted to have dozens of babies with him."

"What did he say?"

"'Sounds like fun', I believe were his exact words."

Dr. Kennedy rolled her eyes. "For him, sure."

"Oh, come on, it's not that bad. You do a little work, and then you get such a wonderful present!"

"Pregnancy hormones have rotted your brain," said Dr. Kennedy, deadpan.

"Takes one to know one," shot back Dr. Rodriguez.

"Mommy look!" said Brad, running up with a box from the crate that was almost bigger than him. "My name's on it! See!"

Dr. Rodriguez saw a piece of paper with 'Bradbury DeSoto Rodriguez-McCracken' typed in a large, clear font had been taped to it. Underneath was a smaller note: "Your turn. Love, your big sis".

It was a drum kit.

Dr. Rodriguez groaned. "Looks like she's still mad about the electric guitar I gave my nephew."

"Maybe Brad will be good at it," suggested Dr. Li.

"Or maybe it will 'accidently' fall down a canyon," joked FirstStep.

Meanwhile, over in the laboratory area of the colony all of the experiments that couldn't wait were being unloaded, cataloged, and set up. Once McGowan, Kalnietis and Dr. Harrington-Murphy had finished helping Dr. Sakai with the plants that had to be immediately moved from the ship to into the hydroponics garden they began going through some of the other high priority level projects sent up.

Kalnietis removed the cryogenics capsule from the rest of the laboratory supplies. "Oh joy, Dr. Nguyen's project is here," he said dully. "I cannot wait for that bright day when we all travel via ice cube trays."

"I agree I wouldn't be too eager to travel that way myself," said Dr. Harrington-Murphy, "but if we're going to get anything bigger than rabbits here, freezing them is the only way to do it."

"Still trying to get clearance for that goat farm?" teased Kalnietis.

"You just watch, it'll be great," said Dr. Harrington-Murphy. "Fresh goat cheese and milk that hasn't been dehydrated and the things can be efficient little garbage disposals and produce fertilizer from it."

"Well, let's see what this brave little volunteer has to tell us about the progress in cryogenics." He made notes on the read out of the capsule, then, table set up, began the decanting process.

"You remember what to do?" asked Harrington-Murphy.

"Yes, yes, I've unfrozen and dissected enough rodent-popsicles to do this process in my sleep by now," said Kalnietis, already impatient to be done. He flicked on the recorder: "One adult male feline, has been in suspended animation for 176 days. Throughout journey vital signs were monitored by capsule, showing all signs that subject was still alive and sustaining on minimal life support. Beginning unfreezing process."

Once out, Kalnietis put the limp pile of fur on the scale, weighing the cat and jotting down more notes and speaking into the recorder about weights and measurements.

"Now to ascertain current heart rate," he stated, and then frowned, brushing at the fur. "We'll need to shave the area to attach the heart monitor." He pulled out a tape measurer from one of the drawers and bent down to measure the hair growth for the record.

He then pawed through one of the drawers, looking for where he had put the razor, not seeing the cat's limbs start to stretch. When he had found the razor and looked back at the table he saw the cat's tail twitching. "Subject is showing signs of muscle control returning," he observed. "It appears to have entered stage three of wake up proc-ahhhhhhhhh!" his academic observations turned into an anguished scream as the cat leaped up and latched onto Kalnietis's front.

With exquisitely sharp little claws, the cat scrambled up Kalnietis to his scalp while Kalnietis flailed his arms and hopped around, screaming in Lithuanian, caught between a scientific desire to get a hold of the subject without damaging it, and a primeval want to destroy the pain-causing-thing. The cat bounded from his head and began to sprint through the lab like a Parkour champion, taking full advantage of the lower gravity to make his escape.

"Get him!" yelled Dr. Harrington-Murphy, already out the door.

"Subject is on the move and clearly in stage five!" yelled Kalnietis for the benefit of the recording, hot on the other's heels.

"Kal," called out McGowan, exasperated, "wait, you're *bleeding*, you idiot!"

In the common area the contents of the crate of care packages from home had mostly been opened and scattered about, some were reading notes from families, candy was being shared around, Dr. Vieira was making the old the-Pilgrims-thought-they-were-far-from-home joke, and overall there was a feeling of Christmas morning after the presents had been unwrapped and the parents were enjoying the second cup of coffee in peace while the kids played with the toys.

Brad actually was showing every sign of interest in the drum kit, despite his mother's efforts to distract him with a number of other - quieter - Hasbro toys. Meanwhile, Anne, happily wearing the red monstrosity over her coveralls, was methodically going through each box and sorting them by a shapes and colors, according to her royal whims, peering into everything hopefully in case anything had been overlooked.

FirstStep came in with snacks, calling out, "Time for high tea, here at the Martian palace." It was just PetriPork on low gravity bread diced up into little triangles with plastic cups of lukewarm lime "iced" tea, but everyone helped themselves with a gusto. Anne grabbed hers and ran back to her box pile where she was concentrated on playing with something in one of the larger boxes.

Kennedy called out, more for the benefit of the camera recording the event than anything else, "What did you find, sweetie?"

"Look! They gave me a kitty!" said Anne, holding something up.

"Oh, that's nice, a furry t- oh shit its alive!" cried out Rodriguez as she saw the cat devouring down the PetriPork that Anne was feeding it.

"No bad words!" lectured Anne.

"No bad words!" said Brad, taking up the refrain.

"No bad words!" they cheerfully chanted together at the grownups.

The cat continued to eat Anne's lunchmeat, ignoring the noise it had caused.

At that point Harrington-Murphy came in, quickly followed by Kalenitis and McGowan, all skidding to a halt in the doorway at the sight of all the adults staring at Anne.

"Has anyone seen a- uh, caaaat-" the last word dragged out as McGowan saw Anne petting the escaped experiment.

Anne looked up at the would-be hunters with a delighted grin and announced: "His name's Sir Purrington," as she continued to feed him from her lunch.

"Oh- *urine bricks* she's named it!" Dr. Harrington-Murphy hissed-screamed.

Kalnietis glanced at the camera, then grinned back at the little girl and said, "That's a great name, princess." He turned to his sputtering colleague, still grinning, all his teeth showing. "Isn't that a great name, Joe? So much better than causing childhood trauma by removal of the subject, right?"

Dr. Harrington-Murphy glanced at the camera and then ground out from between clenched teeth, "Yes. Right. Great."

"Besides, it's hardly a violation of the Prime Directive," Kalnietis added pompously.

"Oh shut up, Spock," snarled Harington-Murphy. "McGowan, please <u>do</u> something with your Trekkie boyfriend!"

She pointed at the Rebel Alliance tattoo on her shoulder. "I've been <u>trying</u> to convince him Star Wars is the better story."

Harrington-Murphy put his hand over his eyes. "Fine, whatever, but one of you is going to send the message to Nguyen explaining what happened to his pride and joy of an experiment."

McGowan and Kalnietis turned on each other. "Rock, paper, scissors, lizard, Spock," they chanted. Lizard poisoned Spock, and Kalnietis sat down at the computer set up for video recording to send a message back to the MECC.

"So hey, Dr. Nguyen, slight hiccup in the cold sleep program," began Kalnietis cheerfully.

Forty million miles away, when Dr. Nguyen finished watching the video, he grabbed at his hair and screamed, "Those damned Kennedy women!"

Author Bio

Kara Race-Moore studied history at Simmons College as an excuse to read about the soap opera lives of British royals. She worked in educational publishing, casting the molds for future generations' minds, but has since moved into the more civilized world of litigation. Ms. Race-Moore attended 6th grade in a one-room schoolhouse on an island, an experience that taught her how to live with limited resources on any planet.

She first came to science fiction through reading Anne McCaffrey's work and is still grateful to her for showing an impressionable teenager that women can be in, and write, science fiction.

Nadia's Rescue

by Dorene McLaughlin

Chilly. That was the first impression everyone got when they visited the clinical rooms of Sandra Cummings' suite of offices. Not that many people frequented her storefront facility, but with the thermostat set at a steady seventy degrees, it welcomed no accidental company.

Most people driving by wouldn't stop anyway; the storefront was one of only five in the rundown strip mall. The sign above said something about legal work or something else so monstrously boring that even a skateboarder who practiced popping ollies for hours a week directly in front couldn't have told you what the sign actually read. Even as it glowed a noticeable red and green at night from leftover Christmas lights, people drove hurriedly by to escape the neighborhood and ignore the half-abandoned shopping plaza. The leftover shop sign, deceptively un-tarnished, did not reveal the true nature of the building's occupants in any case.

It was a miracle Nadia found the chilly offices at all. She'd been looking for something discreet per Sandra's instructions, but she'd never imagined a place so incongruent with her associate's personality. Dr. Sandra Cummings' upbringing and list of letters trailing her name smacked of precision and orderliness, and one could picture a fine straight nose and simple, neat hair without ever having met her. Nadia paused a moment as she swung her heavy handbag onto her shoulder and scrunched her nose to make her glasses slide up. She glanced around the empty lot, not to take in her surroundings as an astute person might have done in a questionable part of town on a dull grey afternoon, but because she waited out of practice for the small figure who emerged from the backseat of the sedan.

When Amelia's feet met some loose gravel made from the cracked asphalt, Nadia knew by sound that her daughter was coming along. She didn't wait to see Amelia's attempt to hurry as she rounded the side of the car nor did Nadia ask if she needed help. There was no malice or intentional neglect in this action. Nadia understood her daughter had needs and in the early years had worried herself silly trying to acclimate her only child to a world of unsympathetic onlookers.

If you asked Nadia, she would be unable to tell you the moment her motherly despair had turned to inner loathing. Perhaps she was even unconscious that she had transformed her need to protect the weak into a type of self-preservation. Years of rolling on a stormy sea had finally given way to piloting her ship for a course, any course that gave life direction. So with thoughtless need to plow ahead, to get *somewhere*, Nadia marched forward to the shaded glass door and pushed the metal bar; Amelia did her best to keep up.

Life looked a bit different for the girl of seven. Short for her age, Amelia was roundish in the middle, similar to her stout mother. Her wobbly carriage rocked toward the now-closed door, the one her mother had passed through. The yellow scarf about her neck trailed to either side of her. This oversized neckwear from her grandmother had been meant as a symbol of sunshine and light for her disabled granddaughter and namesake. "Sunshine" was not a word that immediately came to mind when one spotted Amelia. She wore the long, gauzy material wrapped too tightly about her throat to keep the adult-sized accessory from the flowing to the ground. It made her sweaty and a little out of breath from her rock-walk, rock-walk on one long leg, one short leg to reach the door. But the impudent scarf became a friend as soon as she managed to get the door open. It was chilly inside.

The girl didn't know what to make of the place as she surveyed the empty waiting room with its plain linoleum floors and simple metal, arched-back chairs. She used her hand to push up her glasses, less stylish than her mom's but just as thick. They took up most of her large face and helped detract from the greasy, thin hair that hung wisped by her ears. Uncertainty consumed the cold emptiness before her.

She was alone.

Voices soon echoed in the hallway, a familiar mix of education and civility. By the time Amelia arrived, her mother was in animated conversation with someone she obviously knew. Someone Amelia did not.

Her mother talked with her hands, her back to Amelia, and Amelia didn't know where to look or where to go. She always had the sense that she wasn't quite invited into her mother's conversations but that her mother expected her to be near enough to hear—as if some profound admiration or respect would develop from Amelia's eyewitness accounts of these pontifications. Instinctively, Amelia understood this to be a guileless gesture of Nadia's. Amelia had been lost at sea along with her mother since birth; without a boat of her own to pilot, she was hopefully confident that somehow she would arrive at a better destination if she quietly sat back—

sometimes frightened, often forgotten—and waited for her mother to find control of the helm.

It was the doctor who peered over her mother's shoulders to give arched eyebrows at Amelia as if to say, "And this is…?"

Nadia noticed after a few seconds, missing the social cue few others would. "Oh, uh, yes. Sandra, this is my daughter, Amelia." Her voice did a curious thing at the end of the girl's name. It peeked with a drawn out "ahh", immensely proud of the name she had picked seven years ago, even if the girl hadn't lived up to its expectations. "Amelia, say hello to Dr. Cummings."

Amelia tucked her chin toward her non-existent neck and let the scarf hide her mouth. She twisted a little, side to side. If they had given her one moment more to produce the word, she might have. But her mother couldn't wait for delayed bravery. Her mission was more important; Nadia turned back to the doctor and continued her conversation with eagerness. She had only spoken a sentence and used her fluttering hands twice, before a decisive whine and then a bark brought them all to silence.

A series of answering barks followed, and Dr. Cummings turned to Amelia with a little smile. "You want to see?" Dr. Cummings' face held features so much softer than her mother's. Her wide eyes hinted at intelligence but contained a twinkle that felt friendly. Her smile was welcoming, and Amelia wondered for the first time what this doctor did.

Following the doctor and her lab coat down the hall, Amelia gave a sideways glance into each room they passed.

They were all empty of people. Some rooms looked unused, some had lab equipment and long tables, but none of them showed signs of life. Having spent a childhood in and out of doctor's offices, Amelia guessed they were not in a physician's presence. This new friend of her mother must have something to do with the long hours spent with big books and highlighters, computer screens and printouts, a satchel always overflowing with something meaningful that Amelia could not touch.

The lifelessness ended with intense barking when they reached the large room at the end of the hall. It had been a separate shop in the strip mall conjoined with the destruction of a wall. Now one could enter the added rooms either to the right or to the left. A Plexiglas partition divided the two.

Amelia stayed close to her mother, but both stepped forward with uncertainty. In the room to the left, double-stacked cages sat on a table about three feet high. Every other cage was empty; every other one held a beagle. The dogs were excitedly yapping now and conversation proved next to impossible. Amelia remained quietly intimidated while Nadia waited patiently for a chance to speak again as the doctor prattled on, raising her voice over the din, her manicured hands flicking here and there to punctuate a point. Wordlessly, Nadia kept her own pudgy hands over her generous middle, tucked away as a sign she had no intention of using them for labor. She had come to be handed the research information she desperately sought, not to become part of it.

"So this is where you conduct your trials?" Nadia finally had an opportunity to ask. Amelia had heard that word before and wondered if this meeting had anything to do with her. She stood dumb, not because she was unable to speak, but because over the years she had simply found it easier not to. Her mother's pursuits in psychology had given no insight into Amelia's selected periods of silence until, void of explanation, Nadia instead focused on her studies for study's sake.

Being highly intelligent and vapidly curious about the world, Nadia lost herself in the world of knowledge, not experiences. Continuing education was an easy distraction. And distraction had become a tool, an escape, a weapon. Looking at reality straight-on failed as a survival tactic, so she looked at life through the edges, round the side of her glasses. Adding to her BS in Psychology was just her current distraction, an aimless direction in which to pilot the boat. Nothing more.

Dr. Sandra Cummings closed the partition between the rooms and hallway, successfully muffling the yips from the other side. She turned her back with a lifted chin, an odd sort of pride sliding down her perfect nose into the soft line of her mouth.

"That's it. The CIR I told you about."

Nadia tried to conceal her excitement as she gazed at the device she had spent so much time researching. Sandra's blog had led Nadia to a fast series of communications, ending with a promising invitation to her clandestine lab, and hints of unprecedented documentation.

Sandra walked over and stroked the top of the machine, and if one watched closely enough, one could see a look of exhilaration cross her eyes. "The Cognitive Image Reader has been highly successful in humans, an aid to therapists in tracking trauma patients' pain. Well, their painful thoughts, that is. The neuron signals in their head signals the machine, and the displayed colors represent their emotions. Originally, it was just a tool to study how emotions processed. Nothing more than a visual of what was happening emotionally. But soon therapists found that if trauma victims recognized *when* their emotions were flaring, they could help pinpoint *why* they did. They made connections between events, triggers—all fascinating, don't you think?"

Nadia nodded as if she had been listening while admiring the machine. Fascinating, yes, but she had found published research on the CIR already. She needed something *new* to impress her cohorts, a group of overachievers who had little time for an older, overweight single mother with innocuous looks and an odd, disadvantaged daughter. As the group chased down an original thesis for their latest presentation for the head of the department at the end of the month, Nadia had at last found a way to draw their notice. If what Dr. Cummings claimed was true....

The student followed the doctor around the room, letting her present various machines that meant nothing to Nadia. What they did, how they worked—none of that interested her. The conducted experiments and the data they produced—the thought of a crisp beige manila folder with that information—held Nadia's imagination. She lost herself in wondering where it could be.

In her pining interest, Nadia hadn't noticed her daughter's expression as the girl viewed the caged animals through the glass; nor how she took stock in the machinery that lined the room. It never occurred to Nadia to view her own daughter as an experiment—what she would do or say in this situation or that? What would a disabled girl in second grade say when others made fun of her, for example? Or how did she feel when the teacher consistently favored the blonde girl whose mother ran the PTA over a mousy, abnormally awkward student? Or what would one of her fancy diagnostic charts look like if it considered the odds of a child—bullied and forgotten—to grow? Succeed? Survive?

Amelia pressed her back against the wall and disappeared as Nadia nodded at the appropriate times and held to her patience till the doctor took her to the CIR once more.

"It does more than just help trauma victims," Nadia prompted. "In your email, you said you have—"

"Ahhh… yes," Sandra drew out, her eyes filling with a faraway look. "Dr. Lisa Minoff didn't end with simply using colored graphs. She modified the machine to have an alternative set of needles." She indicated something on the machine that Amelia could not see. "This enables the machine to do more than graph colors. Using an unidentified test subject she got one-of-a-kind results." Sandra paused, seeing that she had her audience of one captivated by the information her painted lips were about to reveal. "She got a *word*. The machine actually graphed *letters*!"

"So, the machine can read human thought? Who was the test subject?" Nadia interjected now, visually impacted by this news. "You have verified documentation of this?"

"Well," Sandra waved a hand mysteriously through the air, "it was just a word."

"Dr. Minoff, you say? Where would I find—"

"It was just a start," Sandra continued, not ready to lose her audience yet. "Dr. Buller's research on animals and neuro-imaging—you're familiar with his work?" Her manicured hand posed mid-air and her perfectly plucked eyebrows arched.

Nadia shook her head.

"Oh, fabulous material. You see it's quite possible that the animals can think and feel like we do. This CIR puts that theory to the test."

Nadia looked around the room again, patiently pretending enthrallment. But after she pushed her glasses up with a wrinkle of her nose, she worked up the courage to say, "Wow. That's really something. To see words graphed from the mind! So… you have some sort of—"

"Want to see how it works?" Sandra smiled her pretty lips past Nadia's lumpy form, and it took a few awkward seconds for Nadia to register that she was addressing Amelia.

The forgotten girl, who had remained silent and still the entire time, slowly shook her head and buried her face again in the yellow scarf. The scarf was more of mustard colored, sometimes brownish in the right light, not at all what Amelia's grandmother had intended. Instead of creating an icon of cheer and hope, Grandma had added to Amelia's

127

image as the girl with the limp and *that yellow scarf*. It gave Amelia sanctuary from the scary world instead of the confidence to challenge it.

"No?" Sandra's head cocked in mild disbelief when Amelia showed no interest in the machine. She was unfamiliar with small girls with two different-sized limbs and what would make them so shy. She shrugged and looked at Nadia for validation. Nadia lips turned up, politely trying to include her daughter in their lift, but her sole focus continued to lay on where the promised documentation could be inside this makeshift lab.

"These probes," Sandra continued touching the small, white suction cups at the end of long red wires, "once attached to the cranium, will activate the CIR. Well, the thoughts will. It's complicated." She rubbed at an imagery spot on the machine. "But the colored graphs are just... well," she waved a hand to show that words were not enough to explain their magnificence.

An unusually loud bark brought the doctor's attention back to the creatures beyond the Plexiglas. "Poor dears," she said, and the further delay finally produced a sigh from Nadia. "They're rescue animals. All of them once owned by a research facility that did God-knows-what to them. Thank goodness I got them. A small price, too. A much better life here. No one can call my testing cruel," she concluded awkwardly. A loud barking that excited the other dogs started up again, and a different kind of look crossed the doctor's face. It evaporated the twinkle that had been there, and the welcome in her smile had gone. "Attaching the probes for a few hours a day doesn't bother them at all.

"Once when using the probes, I got the most rigorous patterns of green graphed," Sandra continued and headed toward the door as if to put an end to their lab tour.

Nadia rushed quickly behind the doctor and out the door. "Really?" she asked. "And what does the color green indicate?"

Amelia never heard the reply as the figures moved down the hall, leaving her alone in the lab. She was uncertain of where to go, what she was supposed to do while she waited, but she no longer found Dr. Cummings pretty or inviting. Waiting alone would be preferable to being asked to respond again.

Yips and barks from behind her moved Amelia away from the Plexiglas. She'd never had a pet and had been to the zoo just once. The unpredictable and self-absorbed mannerisms of animals made her leery of them. Instead, she moved to the inanimate machines ahead of her on tables against the wall, visiting each with a blank stare. She tried to find the fascination her mother had or the importance that the doctor found, but the cold, printer-shaped frame sat lifeless and dull before her. This one was the CRI or RIC?— she had already forgotten its name. Absently, she fingered one of the many suction cup probes, wondering if it held any electrical current. Maybe it worked like one of those things medics put on people's chests when they lay on the ground unmoving. The probes connected to the box, and from its top, motionless graphing needles poised above the paper that fed through it.

She stroked a cup and startled when a needle moved.

Instantly, Amelia released the cup and shoved her hands into the mustard material draped down her middle. The needle stopped; no lines marked on the paper. Amelia took a step back and waited. The needle snoozed.

Amelia turned to the Plexiglas and eyed the dogs in the cages. She wasn't sure what a beagle was, but they knew what a human was, and once she made eye contact, the yaps and whines broke out anew.

Amelia made no indication of feeling.

Glancing toward the door, she considered her options and still couldn't bring herself to follow her mother. Nadia would return for her soon enough. Her mother's distractions kept her at a distance, but Amelia knew she would never abandon her, never give up fighting for them. Lately, she had just been... preoccupied. These animals must have something to do with that, right? Why else would they be here?

Without planning her investigation, Amelia opened the door in the Plexiglas and entered the yapping chamber, the smell more pungent than she remembered from moments ago. Poop and chemical concoctions filled the air with odor. Amelia plugged her nose and moved between the crates, keeping her distance from the creators of the noise and smell. A particularly eager beagle bounced up and down with its forelegs, its back legs locked in place. Each time it came down in the cage, its ears bobbed in a comical fashion that Amelia had never seen. She laughed, and it sent a snort through her plugged nose and out her lips till they sputtered. That made her laugh more, an uncommon sensation for her.

She continued to laugh with her nose plugged and lips sputtering as the beagles looked on. The bouncy one stopped and cocked its head side to side, trying to figure out what manner of human this was.

It was impossible to ignore his soft floppy ears and perfect brown spots, the rambunctious tail cutting through the air like the baton of an overenthusiastic band conductor. More timidly than she had touched the machine probes, Amelia put her finger to the cage and met a small, wet nose. Brown eyes blinked at her and another whine came, followed by a long, pink tongue. Amelia didn't know to be scared, though she had always shied away from dogs. She didn't know to be awed or saddened or to relate in any way to the animal encaged. Had someone told her that she resembled the pup in its thoughts and fate, she would not have been able to comprehend the meaning of it. She could only marvel that for a brief moment there was something more inside her that she ever knew existed there.

With a pure abandonment she had never allowed herself, she wiggled her fingers in the cage holes and let the soft tongue and subtle fur stimulate her. She read the tag above the cage. It had a series of letters and numbers and official-looking date, but in bold print at the top was a single word: **Bailey.** That had to be the name. If Amelia had been an average girl, she would have been cooing the word, sweet-talking to make a new friend. But Amelia had no experience in such things. So she drew closer and closer to the cage using her fingers as the only method she knew to explore the new sensation stirring within.

In the next room, the needles sprang to life.

Amelia heard the needles above the dogs, the high-pitched sing of the graph in operation an odd break in the canine chorus. She moved through the door in the clear wall and watched as several mechanical arms, spider-like appendages, jumped about on the paper. It stopped almost as soon as it started, the squiggly slanted lines difficult to see across the space.

Her feet carried Amelia to the machine to stand over the page, the machine now lifeless. In the scrolling loops and dips that should have been nothing more than zig-zags sat a single word.

hate

For a reason Amelia couldn't explain, her heart began to beat a bit faster. She shivered in the chilly room. The machine's arms jumped back to life and Amelia startled for a second time. More letters formed.

hateme

Amelia didn't move. Her eyes widened with uneasiness. It had become easier to keep her thoughts to herself, but at the moment, she wished she could speak somehow of the fluttering uncertainty that rose in her chest.

The text continued, long lines this time, spread out over the page, letters from one arm connecting with another until two phrases emerged, overlapping and intertwined.

I'm nobody

end me

Amelia took a step backward. Something told her she should go, perhaps tell somebody. The machine sputtered on, needles scratching, arms jumping, frantic and desperate to communicate. The suction cups sat like empty bowls attached to limp noodles beside it.

forgotten
don't want tobehere
end it all
wish I could die

Amelia slowly turned and walked, watching one foot go up and one foot go down, as she faced a turmoil built up over seven long years that a single moment could never reconcile. She stopped at the two doorframes, one leading to the caged room divided off from the lab, one to the hallway. Behind her, the graph stayed busy.

nobody knows
they won't believe me
I can't do this anymore

A glance toward the dogs brought them into full-scale excitement again, and this time Amelia saw them with eyes wide open. Bailey did his funny little bounce, but there was Ricky and Grover, Tiki and Mole, too. The smell seemed insignificant now, and she visited first one cage and then the next, letting each dog lick at her fingers, pressing her cheek against the grid when she could, getting tongue baths, tiny scratches, earfuls of barks, and soft fluffs of fur to linger over. Her heart pounded more wildly, as it filled and emptied with each encounter, until Amelia found herself in the middle of the cages doing the only thing she knew to do with the tide of emotion that threatened to drown her.

She screamed.

Amelia screamed while the dogs went crazy, until she thought her lungs might burst, and after two sets of hurried feet and terrified eyes joined her, she continued to scream without reason, without expectancy, with large tears long past due. But for once, she broke the silent cage she had created even as the machine next door continued to roll.

Amelia had come alive.

**

Nadia's living room, warm and comfortable, did not match Dr. Cummings' attire. The simple sweater over a plain, stretchy skirt did not convey the down-to-earth, relatable personage Cummings was going for. She looked stiff and awkward on the patch of carpet just beyond Nadia's entryway. That was as far as she had been invited in.

The doctor glanced at the folded paper wrinkling within her grasp and tried once more to make herself clear. "The text fills up an entire page. Well, it's fragments, and some are nonsensical, but *words*! Surely you can see how extraordinary that is?"

Nadia bobbed her head, but said nothing. In the back of the house, a joyful bark sounded, fading in and out as it moved.

"I just thought you would want to see—"

"Yes," Nadia's head moved up and down. "I got to see."

"I know you saw that day, but well, the graph continued after you left." Sandra's eyes enlarged as her eyebrows arched with importance. "Here. Take a look."

Nadia let her glasses slide down her nose so that she could

see the piece of paper Dr. Cummings thrust her way. But she made no move to unclasp her hands, tucked up around her large middle in her typical fashion. What a difference forty-eight hours made. Exactly that long ago, Nadia had stood before the doctor and would have given anything for one shred of evidence to take with her. And now, the world's first graph of its kind, the *original* documentation to boot, had showed up at her doorstep.

And she couldn't wait for it to leave.

"I know what it says," the patient Nadia said and wriggled her glasses up. "But thank you for stopping."

Sandra's mouth hung open in disbelief. She shook her head to indicate she did not accept this answer and unfolded the paper before Nadia so she had nowhere else to look.

so mean

please end me

I'm done

they'll never miss me

"I am familiar with the text," Nadia stated again. The words burned her eyes as they had that day in the lab. She lifted her chin a little in an attempt to forget the undiluted cries of her only child that day; she would do anything never to hear them again.

The doctor flinched at this cool reception. The last two days had been a maddening rush of tests and investigations for her. She longed for a reason behind the miraculous graphing, and she tested each dog over and over again, until a sudden visit from the local Animal Angels Rescue group had come to take away her subjects. How the door came to be unlocked she couldn't guess. It was ludicrous that anyone would report her as an unfit guardian. She kept the cages clean, and no dog was undernourished or diseased. They were housed and fed, kept cool and healthy—she had rescued them, for God's sake! But they were gone in a matter of hours, and then it was just her and the silent machine.

"I think," the doctor tried again, not ready to be dismissed, "that perhaps... you are somehow under the impression... that these were Amelia's thoughts?"

Amelia's mother kept her steady feet planted and her smile thin and tight. "It's *your* machine, Doctor. You would know best what happened."

"Well, of course I *don't* know what happened. I wasn't in there!"

"You showed me the video. You saw Amelia touch the probes beforehand. Perhaps she," her hands began to wave here, "messed something up."

The doctor felt her chance and opened the paper again. "Yes, yes, I considered that, but look at these last lines . . .

I need my family
can I go with you
will you tell
save me

"Why would Amelia be asking for her family when you were there?" Sandra's voice rose, begging for affirmation. "Or want to go with someone? She knew you were just down the—"

"Dr. Cummings." Nadia sighed, her tell-tale sign that patience was waning, "you want me to believe that either my daughter, who was not attached to the probes, or the dogs, who also were not in contact, somehow sent thought waves over the air and onto the graph? Is that what you are asking?"

Realization hit the doctor and she took a step back, the paper hanging dejectedly at her side. "And *you* want *me* to believe that you don't believe any of this." Not a question.

More happy puppy sounds broke free from the backyard. The Animal Angels had given their first adoption of beagles to this broken family, a family slowly making its way back to good. The piece of paper filled with hurt and pain that Sandra held so tightly would not be of any benefit to the healing process now underway within Nadia's house.

Nadia gave a dismissive nod and moved around the doctor to open the door. She let Dr. Sandra Cummings walk herself to her car as she turned the lock behind her.

The mother moved through the house quicker than normal now. The new sounds from the back had all her attention. To her right, she passed a satchel, spilling with important articles that she needed to mark and cite for her next meeting. To the left, a wall clock told that it was an hour past time to meet her cohorts for the groundbreaking revelation on thought imaging she had promised them. She noticed neither. They were distractions, after all, and Nadia could only see now what was clearly in front of her.

In the kitchen, Amelia's grandmother—the family's first Amelia—leaned over the island counter, watching her granddaughter play in the backyard. Nadia joined her and they witnessed in awe as a wobbly, short-legged girl did her best to run with Bailey and the equally energetic partner,

Tiki. White fur, brown spots, floppy ears, and a duo of tails, danced and pranced and filled the yard. Both dogs jointly included Amelia, not letting her out of their sight for a second, circling around the grass to convince themselves she was truly theirs. A mustard-colored scarf lay lifelessly on the porch, no longer bound to Amelia's neck.

Laughter carried louder than the barks, a sound that startled both women. The older Amelia realized it could be the first time she had ever heard the noise from her granddaughter—free, unfettered, repetition of long peals of laughter, the kind that comes from pure joy all your own. The exuberance of it made joy bubble into her throat and her own odd, quick laughter burst out. Her hand fluttered to cover her mouth in surprise.

She turned to share her amazement with her daughter and was even more surprised to find a steady flow of tears pouring down Nadia's cheeks.

"Why, Nadia!" she exclaimed. "Whatever is the matter?"

Nadia remained silent for a time, letting the tears flow where the words couldn't. With concern, Amelia reached out a hand to touch Nadia's arm. Nadia patted it back and worked her lips into syllables.

"It's nothing. I was just thinking," Nadia said in gulps. But words, her long familiar friends, now escaped her. The boat she had forced to sail through uncharted waters just to have a direction, a goal, now idly and peacefully bobbed upon an open ocean of possibilities. The distractions floated out of sight. Her daughter no longer sat as a mere passenger behind, but in Nadia's imagination, had moved beside her, an eager co-captain.

Nadia struggled to verbalize the new hope and possibility that overwhelmed her. She finally settled for the simple truth that she knew her mother would grasp.

"It was a good rescue, wasn't it?"

Author Bio

Dorene McLaughlin teaches middle school English, an outlet for her love of discussing and crafting literature. Her passion for the written word overflows into her downtime, where she dabbles with fiction to include a novel that has been in the works for a number of years and the occasional short story. Her writing credits are short and  varied—from greeting cards to magazine articles—but she envisions a future that involves more writing than teaching. Currently, her part-time job involves tutoring college students in essay writing and literature analysis, which she finds stimulating and rewarding.

The Last Dog

by Randee Dawn

The last dog sees her chance and bolts.

She squirms and wriggles and nips until she escapes the rubber-gloved hands and then she is out the van door, a streak of light propelling herself into the road, hind legs pumping across heaved-up concrete, toes gripping broken sidewalk. Her pupils contract in the bright sun, expand in the dark shade. She weaves through stalks of legs, slides past strangers' grasping hands, ignores shouts at her back. Ignores her name.

She will not be going with the people in the van today.

Nor any other day.

A sudden yank as a hand snags on her collar, and her throat closes, tongue shooting forward. Her legs buckle under her belly and she scrabbles, scraping and turning until her head twists through the collar and she is free again, no longer bound to anyone.

She has to be free. She must be let alone. The Next Thing is coming.

Flipping this way, then that way, she rounds bends and corners, vaults steps two at a time, breath slicing in and out with a rasping wheeze as she propels herself through this wondrous, terrifying dreamworld. From every direction come explosive sensations—scents teasing her nose, flashes blinding her eyes, sounds thudding in her ears. She ignores them all; there is no thinking, only *doing* as her paws carry her forward.

Soon, any pursuers' steps fade, grow distant. Are gone.

It has been an incalculable space of time since she roamed the outside dreamworld alone, but even as she pushes her heavy body forward, focusing on putting distance between herself and anyone who might restrain her, she can feel it in her bones: this outside dreamworld is one of less. Of silence.

Still she runs, tongue dry and lolling. She is not yet finished escaping. She intuits the turns like lightning cracking in her brain: *here*, then *here*, then *there*, then *here*. She responds instantly. The crackling grows slower now, so her movements calm. The need to run recedes and she slows into a trot. *There. Here. There.*

Stop here, signals the gray, shining dog in her mind.

In answer, she slips beneath a splintered slab of fencing. Her distended belly scrapes against the cool earth, teats raw and aching at the touch. The other side of the fence reveals a grassy lot packed with weeds that stand taller than her compact, brown-and-white body and provide her some cover. She cranes her neck, sniffing, and catches whiffs of sweetly rotting food, rich, crumbly earth, metallic puddled water, whispers of smoke but not fire, thick, clotted clothing strong with people-scent but no man no woman no human in here. She is safe and alone for now.

Pausing before a splatter of water, she laps quickly, the acrid taste of chemicals unpleasant in her mouth, but she does not stop. Her body shudders from exertion, a chugging engine changing gear. After a few sips of the tangy water, she collapses, splaying each limb wide. The cool earth caresses her nearly-bare, plump belly, and she rests.

Deep within, her body contracts again: the Next Thing is coming soon.

She had whelps once. Remembers their nuzzling,

chewing, sucking, hot little muzzles pressing into her. Remembers them as they emerged, soaked and wriggling and unscented. Without meaning. Without Story. They might have come yesterday or they might have come a hundred yesterdays ago: she cannot measure time. She knows only that they were with her for a period, and then they were taken by humans dressed in white with rubber coverings on their hands. She is calmed by knowing that all that happened in the dreamworld—and if she wants to see the pups again, all she need do is close her eyes. There, they wait for her.

In time, she lowers her head to her white forepaws, ears pointed and circling, alert. Soon they too droop, her eyes flutter and she dozes, escaping into her realworld.

***

Sleep brings her to the realworld. She enters a tremendous den, a patchwork construct of memory and sense that only she can navigate and interpret. Each patch is a part of her waking dreamworld, a memory she can recall, stitched carefully against dozens of others. The quilt of her memory forms walls, a roof and a floor. Here she can roll around and find everything she wants and be forever happy, sated, secure.

Right now, she is atop a memory of sun. She has rolled over into the brightness, flat belly exposed, legs loose and flopped and someone is petting her. The woman's hand runs up and down her ribcage, over her stomach; her voice making singsong noises. The last dog's tongue flops out one side of her mouth. Eyes are bright and eager for the Exciting Thing she is expecting. Then the hands take hold of her forepaws, manipulating them this way and that and she cranes upward, nipping playfully at the woman's fingers. She falls back and gives in wholly to being spun and tackled by this enormous, gentle creature. Her heart swells full; they are paired and of the same pack, and she knows who she is and who the woman is, and all the scents around them give comfort.

Then she is up on her short legs and bowing forward, nose to the ground. A ball flashes at her—the signal to run—so she chases the thing across the room, down the hallway, nails slipping skidding on the smooth dark floor and snap—the ball is hers. She returns, head held high, legs prancing, joy in her heart and hoping a treat is in the offing.

She knows this patch of memory well; it is one she often visits first when the realworld opens to her, but it is far from the only one she houses there. There are darker memories in this quilt, far out on the edges, of hands that were not kind and caressing, of needles and burning, of long, lonely hours in a too-small cage where she could barely turn around. Those memories are part of her patchwork, despite her desire to forget, and it is only recently that they have begun to be crowded out by the good ones. She skirts around those memories and does not visit them, not if she can avoid it.

Instead, these days, as she dozes the familiar comes to her and runs its fingers over her body like the hands that rubbed her belly and the voice that cooed at her, and she is safe knowing that everything in this memory den has already happened. It is only in waking that she fears new things. In that world she exists in unknown, intrusive territory. She must remain alert.

It is only when she opens her eyes that she fears.

***

A truck jounces on an uneven road beyond the fence, and the last dog, as she thinks of herself now, is jolted into the dreamworld again. She lifts her head in alarm: she is still outside, still alone in the silent, empty lot. The day has warmed, and the puddle she lapped from earlier has drained.

She rises gingerly to her feet, ears cupping at the air. Wind rustles the tall weeds around her; in some far distance, music slides out an open window. Nearer still she hears murmurs, sirens wailing, doors breaking open and slamming shut. Abstract sounds, nothing to do with her.

Bending to the ground, she pushes her extraordinary wet nose forward, probing. The dreamworld is full of so much to smell, and she breathes in. This is the only language in which she is fluent. She knows from one sniff that under this dirt is more water; if she digs for an unknowable time she might jump into a pool of it. Another sniff and she understands she is not alone as she'd thought: three rats and a single raccoon lay somewhere in this lot, aware of her presence but hidden. When she raises her muzzle slightly she clues in on the blood of an animal carcass neither new nor old in a corner of the lot, and a mostly empty bag of what is likely popcorn a short distance from where she stands. She takes in so much with just a few breaths, she must stand still to absorb and process it all.

And yet.

For all the sensations, it is a silent place, absent of Story. There are no messages, no chapters, no information from

147

her scattered pack at all. She roams at random, nose deep in the crisping grass, searching. But no, just like everywhere else, the messages are gone. There have been no signs, or alerts, or notices in all the walks she has taken in all the yesterdays she can recall. The past may be an unformed concept to her, but her memories of the realworld remind her that there have been days before this one, a time when parts of the Story were painted everywhere—on buildings, under rocks, coating tree bases, shimmering in the air. Message upon message, whole conversations and chapters of the Big Story. Some are complex tales, some simple and yearning—flares sent up in a new place, hoping to find listeners. Some messages come full-throated and powerful, others more a timid whisper. All are rich and full of light and sound and instruction. All contain truth and lies.

Smells are how dogs know one another, her mother once conveyed. Markings are messages that allow dogs to access all parts of the Big Story: Are we loved? Do we eat? Where are we in pain? Are we alone? What do we wish for? What guidance do we require? It is the canine tapestry of the one Story all dogs share, and each is a scriptwriter of memory.

During her time with her mother, the last dog learned how every day the entries are diminished by rain or weathering or destruction, but then are quickly replenished once the storm passes, rewritten and reshaped and retold as dogs venture back into the world to start the telling again. The Story always begins again.

Scent is life itself; it is how she connects. She grew up learning to anticipate the next chapter of the Story, brought to her by the exquisite perfection of her nose. She grew up on a Farm, then was taken to the dark place with the cages, and after that to the City. Here she has learned how to live in a different kind of pack—a distant group, one that never meets in toto but is like a family forced to live apart. Finding such messages helps her understand who she is, where she stands, who her alpha is and who she is alpha to. It is the one thing they have that binds all dogs together, this divine part of themselves that is theirs alone.

She longs now for any place where a scrap of Story exists. Even here, in this weedy lot left to its own devices, she finds nothing. Her kind does not speak here; there are no Stories, no voices, no scents at all to mark the landscape. The silence hurts her head, pierces her chest. She roams the lot this way and that, led by random sparks that light up her mind. She traces the perimeter and noses at a spindly tree in the center. Leaves her own poor entry there: a message of desperation she can only hope someone will read before the next storm.

I did warn you, says the sleek, shining dog in her mind. *It is up to you, now. You are possibly the last dog. You must take care.*

Then she finds the carcass she sensed earlier: it is a shaggy, reddish dog, and it does not breathe. Its paws are raw, crusted with dried blood. She sniffs it, but finds nothing but the metallic scent of its feet. It is as if the dog is not even there. She noses it from behind once, then taps its muzzle with a paw. The dog is like stone, solid and heavy and cold. She taps it again and an ear cracks off, then breaks into pieces that crumble instantly into powder, as if the dog were made of something very fragile.

Something is happening to us, the gray dog told her. *We are becoming dust. It is a sickness, and it started with the white coat people, so run from them at all costs. Bite if you must, but always run.*

She backs away from the red dog until she can no longer sense it. Eventually, she comes upon a half-dug hole and draws her claws against it, widening the space and shaping it to her size. She curls inside with a muted whimper of fear and disappointment. Resting her muzzle across one hind leg, she closes her eyes and shifts out of the dream and into the realworld she prefers.

***

She was not always the last dog. She had no idea such a thing could be. Even now, she is only the last dog she knows of, the last dog she knows that lives.

What she does know is that once there was Story everywhere, with infinite new entries. Then the entries began to slacken, with chapters more widely spaced out and not replenished after the rains. The dogs disappeared, and so did their Story. They became dust.

Asleep, she rolls onto the memory of what life was like before things began to fade, the remembrance of her last days on the Farm.

On the Farm, the entire world burst with every scent imaginable, the land covered with waving, prickling grasses, and she ran with a pack of her brothers and sisters, nipping at one another's heels. There was so much to see and do and smell and taste, she would collapse at the end of a day and build her memory den with the richest, deepest, shiniest, heartiest, tastiest. Everything was for the first time, and the new trickled down her throat and nourished her soul.

Then one day she was sent off. The people tried to explain why she must go; she could smell their worry and anxiety and heard sadness in their thin, quavering voices and thickly veined hands, but no matter what they said it was not part of a Story she could read. So she stared at them as long as she could while they packed her in a crate and strangers in white coats stacked her in a van among other whining, scratching dogs.

Then came the bad days.

The crate became her new world; she was rarely out of it for more than a short time, spending her days surrounded by dozens of other similarly trapped animals. Hands with strange smells and coverings reached in from time to time and carried her to a smooth, shiny table and held her down as she was probed, poked, and injected. She would sleep suddenly and wake up with some of her fur gone on one leg. Or a tooth missing. Or a plastic cone around her neck.

In time, there were fewer animals in the room with her. And then fewer still. And one day the people did not come, and she was thirsty and hungry and whining and clawing at the cage. A second day passed, and the stench around her was unbearable. Escape into her realworld proved impossible.

One night the room opened and new hands came, and they did not have white coats, but they took her from the cage and wrapped her and the few remaining dogs in blankets and ran out into the dark, into another van without cages. They took her to a new home in the City where no one poked or prodded or *injected. Here things became good again.*

Her fur grew back. The hands on her once again felt kind. She began rolling over and offering her belly again, letting them know she loved them. There was a man and a woman, and they were good to her. This was a good dreamworld.

But the City was different.

It was a place of suspicious stranger dogs led around on tethers, of more indoor than outdoor life, where she had to understand her new pack's dynamic with a sniff here, a scratch there, always pulled along by her new humans to another place before she was ready, cringing from the booming, wheeled metal boxes that hurtled across the grass-free spaces just inches from her nose.

She became so caught up in her new dreamworld that at first she did not realize that the Story around her was changing. The entries grew less frequent, further apart on the ground, and the messages were fainter, harder to interpret, full of questioning. But perhaps that was just how this new dreamworld worked, she supposed. It was not the Farm. It was the City.

In her first few weeks in the City, she visited her realworld often. Her new people built her a special structure in the corner of one room, and from that sleeping place they let her doze and doze and doze. She dived into the old scents and chapters, and she was once again among her pack in the memory den, dazzled by sunlight and free to wander without a tether, discovering all the Story she could absorb.

In time, she came to adore her new people, but was heartsore for the Farm places she visited in her realworld memory den. Her new people could not understand. They just shrugged and let her do as she liked, so long as she came when they called.

With time, however, the messages on the outside no longer changed—they vanished. She found fewer and fewer, so on her daily walks she would pull to explore further, try and find any scrap of Story that might be left in some corner, down some secret hole, under an unknown bush.

She began to realize this affected more than just her new home. This was about the entire Story. She began to plead for more frequent, longer walks, sitting in front of the door and staring at her people until she wore them down. Outside remained terrifying and noisy and charged, but she had to know. Her pack—her new, scattered pack—was going away and not inviting her to come along. And the few messages she did receive were telegraphing something urgent and terrifying.

Dust, *they all said.* We are dust. There is a sickness, and it is ours.

Then she first heard the shining, sleek dog in her mind and first entertained the idea of being free again.

***

She awakens in the dreamworld, this noisy outside place gone scent-silent. Her ears are keen to every twitter, every shuffle, growl, hiss, thunk, and there are so many here it has taken her a long while to know how to filter them the way she does with scents. To interpret what she must respond to and what she can ignore.

Her belly cramps. Not hunger; she ate not so long before her mad dash from the new van. But a hitching tells her the Next Thing will be very soon, and she must prepare. The last dog stands in her dug-out trench and peers around the lot until she locates what she needs. Taking a deep sniff of a stained, blue fleece blanket—scents of small people, stomach bile, sharp sweet fruit—she clamps onto an edge with her teeth and drags it into the hole. She was alone the one other time this happened on the Farm, her pack running elsewhere and leaving her to complete the panting, heaving, pushing, but she managed. The grass around her was thick and soft, and she found it easy to roll around and create a bed of the stalks on which she could lay and finish her work. So she has done this before; in these moments of necessity, all other worlds disappear, and she is always the last and only dog.

She noses the blanket around until she can lay her body flat against it and begins gasping, the engine starting up again, preparing. She waits for the Next Thing to happen. Her eyes flutter, and she is half-in, half-out of the dreamworld.

***

Her new people loved her, so they gave in to her whimpered requests and stubborn refusal to move from the door until they took her for walks. She darted into the world on a mission, nose low and searching, searching. The messages she found outside were jumbled and confused and questioning. They echoed her own mind: Where are we? Why are we not here? Where are we going?

Her people let her take the lead, and she could feel their confusion in her driving need to press onward, forward, away. She let the charges in her head fly wild so they turned this way and that way and a new way and a further new way until she was taking in messages and chapters from packs she had never scented before but the messages were all the same: We are confused. We are small. We are afraid. We are gone.

One day she found the tree. It stood in a park surrounded by patchy grass and sticks and garbage, populated with distracting squirrels and birds. But it called to her as if it were on fire. She arrowed directly at the tree until her person came along in hopsteps, and she circled it around and around and around, planting her paws on the trunk to take in the messages left higher up. The tree shone so bright, coursing with stories and thoughts and entries, messages so numerous and layered her ears stood bolt upright, her nose alight, her tail stiff and quivering.

One entry, more urgent than the rest, repeated by many, shouted at her.

We are fading, *it said.* Our time is nearly over here. Our Story is ending. Be easy in your mind. Let the change come. We will all soon be in our realworld. Our time in the dreamworld is waning. Do not fight. It is not a bad thing. The Story is nearly complete. It is not our fault. We were all Good Dogs.

This was, at last, new information, that the Story had an ending after all; she had always thought it went on and on like the dogs that pursued their own tails, racing for the sake of the chase rather than an end goal.

Her mind quieted. Answers made it possible to feel less anxious, alone, and frightened. If this was how it was, if this was how the pack had decided, she would go along. As she had submitted joyfully to the humans who gently wrestled with her, she would not fight.

The walk home after the tree was gentler, and she sensed her human was relieved that she had stopped fighting so hard. They came to a new part of the road, and the man paused to poke at a small device in his hand.

Then she spied the gray dog.

He was the first dog of any kind that she had seen in a long while, and he startled her. The dog stood on the sidewalk nearly a block away and had no person. He was magnificent, a thin, glowing, dark gray animal twice her height with a narrow face; shining of eye and short of hair, with tall, pointed ears and a tail curled across his back. She glanced up at her person, who was still tapping on the small, bright square, inattentive.

She bolted to the dog, slipping her collar, a missile with no other thought in her head but that she must reach it and nose it and see if it knew anything. It was a dog-shaped hole in the world, waiting for her and her alone, like an image she saw in her memory den.

She halted, and they gently touched noses. The other dog blinked and held fast for a breath, then ducked and turned around and around with her as they greeted each other. This close reading she had missed after so very long, and her heart thudded with pleasure as she opened her mind to read his signals. He spoke to her in a tumble of gestures and scents and sounds no one but they could hear. He said:

The tree is a lie. We are vanishing, that is true. But we have not been called elsewhere. Do not let the story fool you. It is for whelps to keep them from whimpering.

Once, the Story told us how there were so many of us that the people prevented us from making more. Once, we were so numerous the humans threw us away in sacks filled with rocks that sank to the bottom of the water, or locked us in rooms with poisoned air. Our children drowned, our ancestors suffocated. We were so plentiful we might have run this world, but we chose not to. That part is over. We are changing.

It began in closed rooms with our kind shut away and tested and used for no purpose, and it has grown. They have given us a sickness, and it is changing us. Most humans do not perceive this yet. Some do, and a great confinement has begun for all of us who remain. You will likely be kept inside after today.

Why is this happening to us? We have been Good Dogs. But it is so: All Stories end, even the Big Story. Other creatures once roamed this world, and some of their great Stories ended—there were fewer and fewer of them until they could not make more, and they were gone. When we go, there will be no more memory den. We will leave this dreamworld and go into the earth and think and feel no more.

The message ran through her mind like cold water down her throat, and she stood at attention before him, eyes meeting in understanding. She told him she knew of the rooms and the abuse. She had seen it happen. Her fur was taken.

Must we go with our tails tucked? *she asked him.*

His tail wagged furiously. No, *he told her.* We can still fight. We can refuse.

Yes, *she said, and they touched noses.*

In one swift motion, they ducked together through a set of bushes and behind one of the tall, brick buildings, and he was on her in a flash, bent over her back and nipping at her ears. By the time her person came thundering down the alley toward them, the sleek gray dog had finished, nosing at her face.

We will not meet again, *he conveyed.* Protect your realworld. Protect your whelps, if they come. Find others, if they exist. Be the last dog until you know better.

With that he bounded clear, dashing around the corner, curled tail close to his body. Her person arrived then and scooped her in his arms, nuzzling at her neck and alternately cooing and admonishing. She did not care; her mind still buzzed with a riot of sensations and considerations. Her ears smarted from the gray dog's teeth, but she did not mind the pain. She only wished they might have slept alongside each other, the smallest kind of pack. She soothed herself by taking his memory into her realworld den, knowing he would be resident there forever. She could see him that night.

But she never saw him again in the dreamworld.

She never saw any more living dogs after that.

***

The Next Thing has begun, and she snaps to attention.

The last dog shudders and whimpers, biting at the filthy blanket, her body not her own. The dream dogs inside her now twist and turn and make her belly hard and taut. Time draws out into forever as the sweet agony comes and convulsions wrack her. She dives nose-down into the heaving quiver of her torso, legs extended, tail held high.

She slips briefly into the realworld, lost in a trance again while the Next Thing takes over.

***

The gray dog was right; her people did not take her outside again after that day. They did bring her to a kind of outside at the top of their building, and high in the sky she would send her nose into the air and low into the corners but could hear and smell and read nothing; all was blank and void. She left as many messages as she could up there, but she knew in her heart they were signals to no one.

Inside she paced, anxious. Her people petted and cuddled her as they always had, but she sensed a crackle of change in the air, a cool, dark worry in their gazes that transmitted whenever they touched her head, her fur, her paws. Her food also changed; she began to eat as her people did, and this made her joyful. No hard kibble or soft, mealy meat from a can. Yet with this change came a colder, darker concern, and more restrictions.

Once, certain she had heard a call from her scattered pack, she leapt up on a soft piece of furniture and leaned on the windowsill to peer outside. It proved a difficult maneuver by then; she was filling up with dream dogs, but it had been so long since she had heard her own, native sounds that she had to investigate.

One of her people ran after and pulled her down from the window, silencing her yelp of greeting and held her close. There was much caressing then, a long bout of nuzzling and soft words she could not understand. It began to feel like when her people on the Farm said their goodbyes, down to that long, knifelike blade of worry and fear and sadness.

Few visitors came to the home anymore. When they did, her

people shut her up in a wire den, the door locked and everything tucked away deep in a tiny, dark room. This did not concern her; she could curl up and visit her memory den for a time, but she could never understand why—if she heard voices in her dreamworld—she could not warn or greet. That she had to remain hidden and secret and alone.

Then came this very morning. A new person came to the home, and she was not shut up. Not taken to the upstairs outside. Not hidden. This person came cloaked in an array of smells, old, fragile scents that seemed to dissolve under her nose as she dived around and under and among him, breathing deeply of his clothing and hands and hair. This person had known her scattered tribe, had touched them and been with them—but the parts of the Story he carried to her were like matted fur, tangled, unyielding, old. Still, she was so excited for any new entries or chapters, she leapt and bounded as if she was not a swollen thing carrying dream dogs given to her by the gray dog with a curled tail. She was just a whelp herself again with this new, scent-heavy person.

The person handled her. He looked into her mouth and palpated her belly and stuck something cool and smooth into her backside, but his voice was like burbling water, and she relaxed under his hands while her people watched on nearby. Their chilly anxiety had receded yet also intensified, like one of those high-up white dots in the night sky outside. The last dog whimpered and tried to nose at their hands, but then the tether was clipped onto her collar while the new person spoke in low, careful garble to her people.

The last dog was too excited to pay much attention. All she knew was that outside beckoned. Outside was happening! Where the Story lived, she hoped.

She squirmed and wagged so hard, there was so much happiness everywhere.

Then her people leaned in and touched her face and put their mouths on her head and spoke soft words while their faces grew wet. She licked at them, lapped up that saltiness, tail shifting all the while, eager for her release. Her people grasped her paws and she was swallowed up in cloth, held tight against the new, Story-draped person's chest, so tight she could barely breathe. Then she and the new person left, and her people stayed behind making their own kind of soft yelping.

The new person held her too close but spoke kindly, so she stilled, waiting for what was going to happen. The Next Thing was near then. The dream dogs were coming out and she would need a safe place.

She would need to be free.

The tether was unclipped when the person took her into the back of a new van. A new van like the old van, filled with cages. But this time the cages lay empty.

Hands covered in rubber, hands owned by humans in white coats, reached for her.

The last dog saw her chance, and bolted.

***

The dream dogs are outside her now, all three of them greeting their dreamworld in a gush of hot, wet saltiness and mewling. Each comes out on its own in a push of pain and delight. They smell exactly as she does, until she licks and licks and licks at these bright, hot, twisting dreams, uncovering their squinted eyes and tiny paws. They are gray and white and brown and like tiny versions of herself and the gray dog together, with grasping mouths and teeth that she helps guide to her teats so they can suck and be still.

She is exhausted from her run, her digging, and the Next Thing, but she cannot go into her realworld den just yet; she must ensure her whelps are cared for in this hard dream place, the place they will eventually learn to escape from so they can live in the memory dens they will construct with their own chapters and stories and episodes.

A charge flashes across her mind, and she begins sniffing at them, hard and deep. They are blank canvases, no Story at all attached. They come only with the scent she knows best: her own. But as the minutes pass and they drink deeply of her, that shifts and swirls and changes.

One of the pups bobs his head at her—his eyes are not yet open, but he seems to feel her. He leaves off eating for a short time as they stare at each other, and then she can see the Story begin to unfold on him, an experience fresh and different from her own. She smells deeply of him, takes the scent into herself.

He returns to her belly, and in time the others, both girls, raise their heads to acknowledge their mother. They move together, these two girls, one almost solid brown and the other almost solid white, and they seem to want to tell her something. They look at her, and she hears the gray dog's mind.

Tell them the Story, she hears. *Bring them to the tree when they can walk, and let them learn. They can start the Story over. But take care. You have rescued yourself. You must not let them catch you again. You are of the world now, and yours may be the only pack that exists. They will guard you just as you must guard them. Tell the Story. Tell it all.*

Then the girls return to their meal.

In a future time she cannot measure, the last dog knows she will do this. People are no longer important to this chapter of the Story. This chapter must be written by the survivors, the ones who did not crumble into the ground. Who will not allow themselves to become dust.

She glances over her pups, now sated and breathing and taking their first trip to the realworld. They are seeing their own memory dens for the first time. She sighs. She can rest now, at least for a bit. Before the work of this hard dreamworld begins again.

The last dog—no longer the last dog at all—closes her eyes, tumbles into sleep... and *lives*.

Author Bio

Randee Dawn is a Brooklyn-based journalist and writer of speculative fiction. Her work has appeared in publications including *Fantasia Divinity*, *3AM Magazine*, and the anthology *Children of a Different Sky*. As an entertainment journalist she regularly writes for

Photo credit: Stephen Lovekin

Today.com, Variety, the *Los Angeles Times* and *Emmy Magazine*. She is the co-author of *The Law & Order: SVU Unofficial Companion* and a collection of short stories, *Home for the Holidays*. For more, find her at randeedawn.com and @randeedawn on Twitter.

Two Dogs and a Pig

by Dennis Maulsby

The Irish born Father Donahey has retired from many years of service as a Catholic priest in South American countries to Winterset, Iowa. It's not to be the life of books and long rural walks that he expects. The community and the surrounding area are awash with supernatural creatures. Some friendly, some not, but all must be dealt with in order to protect his new tate, country, and the wider world from chaos and destruction.

Father Patrick Ignatius Donahey and his blonde-haired companion stood on the back steps of the church rectory in Winterset, Iowa. In the yard, two black and tan dogs dodged, rolled, and caracoled in the eight-inches of snow left by yesterday's January blizzard. Chunks of white stuff flew back from their paws.

Donahey squinted and said, "They look a bit large based upon my recollection of Airedales. The male must be all of fifty-five kilos."

Katherine Mary Shelly gave him a grin and a wink. "Good guess, Father. He clocks in at one hundred and twenty five pounds. The female is twenty pounds lighter."

The dogs rose on their hind legs and pawed each other in the chest. Their breath expelled in white puffs of vapor. Falling back to all fours, the female nipped the male on his lower lip and bounded off, closely pursued.

"Kath, are these two some great experiment you're perusing up there at the Vet lab in Ames?"

She waved a hand at the dogs, "Close, Father. We're not

breeding them for size. They are Oorangs, raised exclusively in the States since the early 1900's and naturally large. However, we've done some things with their genetics that I can't discuss, but mainly we are working on canine-computer interface."

Delaney envisioned a cable running from a laptop to plug into the dogs' skull. "Do they have, what do you call them, 'ports?'"

His five-foot-four companion laughed, a pleasing, silvery tinkle. Kath punched his shoulder. "Oh no. They carry a tiny computer inside them. It's inserted under the baggy skin of their ruff. Bluetooth technology allows us to communicate using radio waves."

He felt a chill run through his body. "Do we have *skiborgs*. Are they dangerous?"

"You mean cyborgs? Well, nothing extreme. We use an iPad." She pulled a device from her jacket pocket. Kath clicked it on and swept long fingers over its surface. Little icons appeared.

She held up the nine-inch diagonal screen. "This first app allows us to track the dogs through the GPS device in their implant. We can also communicate with them in primitive ways through low wattage electrical pulses. There is a lot of additional potential to explore, but most of what we are doing is classified. This is a project funded by the Department of Defense's subdivision known as The Defense Advanced Research Projects Agency."

Donahey furrowed his brow and tilted his head. Computers and all their ramifications did nothing but confuse him. His life of service in the backwaters of South America left him little experienced with current techno-society. He stuffed his hands in his parka pockets as though to refuse to touch something that was beyond him. Kath caught the look and posture.

"Father. You've already volunteered to keep Pal and Sal for the next two weeks while I'm at a conference. You can't back out now. Here, I'll show you, it's easy."

Father Donahey watched as she demonstrated how to turn the iPad on and off. She showed him the two icons he would need. A touch on the first one and an overhead satellite map appeared. He could recognize the church. At its rear, two little stars blinked on and off. They mimicked the dogs' play.

When activated, the other icon, shaped like a dog whistle, sent out a recall signal. Kath touched the symbol. The dogs stopped their fun and raced toward the back steps. Pal skidded to a halt and stuck his melon-sized head in Donahey's crotch. The priest jumped and pushed the head away.

"Bejiggers, I hope he doesn't do that every time."

Kath laughed and said, "He just likes you. That was an invitation to play. So, things you should know about Pal and Sal. They are three years old, which is the equivalent of twenty-eight in human years. They are excellent field dogs. Their hard wiry outer hair allows them to slip through brush. A soft short undercoat sheds water."

"Looks like they require a lot of exercise."

"True, but you can let them run and use the recall when

you've had enough." She paused to make sure the Father was paying attention. "To continue, the breed has been used to hunt big game or as family guardians. They are friendly, but are fearless when aroused. They have a very high pain-threshold and can take a lot of damage and still get the job done."

"Will they chase other animals? I don't want the local farmers on my back."

"Just use the recall button if they misbehave. They will stop what they are doing and return."

Donahey caught Kath looking at her watch. Her ride to the Des Moines airport was waiting. "Anything else I need to know?"

Kath frowned and waved a finger over the screen. "Father, you must promise me to use only these two icons. Do not activate the others."

Donahey gave her a wink. "I hear and obey. I hope that Pal, Sal, and I will become close friends."

His companion widened her eyes. "I think you will. Teddy Roosevelt said, 'An Airdale can do anything any other dog can do and then lick the other dog, if he has to.'"

Kath kneeled and hugged the black-saddled terriers. Donahey sniffed, Pal and Sal's odor smelled like other canines he had known, a smoky, musky scent with frilly overtones of meat-based food and dog poop.

***

Father Donahey sat in his favorite wingback chair, finishing an after dinner coffee spiked with his favorite Templeton rye. His canine companions lay on their beds eyes drooping. A week had passed and Donahey had to admit he and the dogs were getting along much better than he had anticipated. He fellow priest had laid down the law, the dogs could sleep in Donahey's office and take their meals in the kitchen, but the rest of the rectory was off limits.

The Airedales were friendly to church parishioners and neighbors, although they had treed that snooty Clara Murphy's Persian tom. The cat loved to leap out of bushes and attack the ankles of passing pedestrians. Well, it would not try that again soon. The dogs chased the cursed critter twenty feet up into a treetop. Donahey had never seen dogs that could leap so high.

Best of all, they enjoyed, as much as he did, long jaunts into the fields and woods of the surrounding countryside. By instinct, or training, or both, the pair would zigzag twenty to fifty feet in front of him, exploring the snowy terrain. When he turned, they raced to get in front of him again. It was good they were so attentive. Today, he had forgotten to charge the battery on the iPad and the recall signal could not be sent. However, his calls had brought them to him. The device, now plugged in, lay on the side table.

Picking it up, he studied the screen. Some nine icons arranged in three rows stared back at him. The promise not to activate the other icons was already broken. Somehow, on day one at that, he had accidentally pushed a symbol shaped like a camera when pulling the iPad out of his pocket. Two choices came up: large X's marked Ch.1 and Ch.2. In a panic, he had touched the screen. A moving picture came up.

171

***

Snow-covered grass and bushes flashed by. A snuffling sound came from a hidden speaker. After a moment of confusion, he connected the changing pictures with the movement of Pal. A color TV camera and microphone were integrated into the dog. The picture stopped and the camera focused on a pile of brown, golf ball-sized objects. Sniffing came from the speaker. Across the bottom of the iPad, a moving bar, like those on the news channels, displayed a message: *Scent identified, White Tail Deer poop.*

"Wow!" Father Donahey said aloud. The connection to the Defense Department became clear. Among other things, these dogs were designed to be military scouts. What they saw, heard—and smelled—could be transmitted back to a handler. A patrol using these creatures would rarely be ambushed.

Pal came on point. The picture on the miniature screen froze. Centered in the screen, a male pheasant cocked its head and gave the dog a beady-eyed stare. The bar at the bottom of the screen flashed and read: *Identification complete: Chinese ring-necked pheasant.*

The image dissolved in a blur as the dog leaped forward. The bird exploded into the sky. Donahey looked up in time to see the sun catch the iridescent copper, green, and red of the cock's breast, head, and wing feathers. The sight never failed to make him catch his breath, the bird caught in a moment of exquisite beauty. Sal and Pal pursued. The pheasant dropped into the cornrows of an adjacent field.

Donahey didn't think the dogs would catch it. The bird would land, dodge left or right, and run as fast as a horse.

After much fumbling, the priest had managed to reset the device by shutting it off and turning it on. He hit the recall and the trio ambled home.

***

Donahey took another sip of coffee. He studied the other symbols. One was shaped as a globe with tiny continents, obviously the earth. The craving came over him to explore. He felt guilty. Oh, well, he thought, in for a penny, in for a pound. He had already taken a risk with the camera icon, might as well go all the way. Tapping the sphere brought up a small numerical keypad and a drop-down menu of two items: **Go to** and **Return**. Touching **Go to** produced two boxes entitled: **Lat.** and **Long.**

His mind leaped. Entering a series of latitude and longitude coordinates would allow the computer to direct the dogs to specific locations. He envisioned them scouting enemy positions or packing fifteen to twenty pounds of supplies to friendly troops.

He returned the screen to the start point. Two other icons appeared to be programmed. One was a Red Cross, or first aid symbol, and the other—a rifle with a bayonet. Donahey looked at the two dogs slumped on their beds. Both relaxed after exercise and a good meal. Their eyes drooped in half-sleep. He raised a finger. His heart began to beat faster. A touch on the rifle icon and a safety question came up:

Activate attack mode? Yes □ No □.

Suddenly alert, Pal and Sal's heads popped up. Eyes opened wide. Ears went flat against their heads. Two-inch claws extended, cat-like, from their toes. Lips pulled back. Jaws opened, exposing rows of key-sized pointed teeth. For a moment, he thought he was looking into alligator mouths. The animals appeared to have bigger and more than the usual number of teeth. Donahey shuddered and stabbed the iPad off button. Claws retracted, mouths closed. The dogs relaxed and lay back.

***

Father Donahey's bottom felt tingly from setting too long on the rough bark of a long-fallen walnut tree. The two dogs sat in front of him, ears up and reddish-pink tongues hanging out the sides of their mouths. Their combination of quivering bodies and excited facial expressions clear signs of begging to be released to run and explore.

For their outing today, he had borrowed the Church's old, rattletrap, 1956 Ford 100 pickup. The faded, red vehicle had rusted out door panels and blossoming oxidation spots on its chrome, but it started every day, huffing and puffing oily bluish-gray breath. Eight years its elder, Donahey felt sympathy for the aged vehicle. He and the truck both needed new parts and a cosmetic work over.

Man and dogs side-by-side in the cab traveled five miles south from Winterset on Millstream Avenue to Clanton Creek Recreational Area. The park's one-thousand-plus acres were kept pristine, with only pedestrian traffic allowed in its combination of woods, savannah, and tall-grass prairie.

"Shake," he commanded.

Pal lifted his right paw. Donahey's fingers squeezed the flesh surrounding the middle toe. A silvery looking spike two inches long pushed out. He ran his thumb across its edge. "Ouch," he exclaimed. A thin line of blood appeared on the skin of the digit. The talon, or whatever it might be, was sharper than the blades of his favorite multi-bladed, stockman's knife.

He raised the paw closer to his sixty-seven year old eyes. In circumference, it was about three-quarters as wide and long as his own hand. Considerable webbing between the toes made for a good swimmer and would help support the animal's weight on snow. He wondered again exactly how the animals would be used. His sense of ethics rebelled at the thought of them being used in warfare. Yet, dogs had probably been the first creatures to be suborned by men. If humans had to kill and destroy, let them do it to themselves, and leave God's other creations in peace.

Pal and Sal's ears snapped to attention, their heads cocked and turned left. Donahey held his breath. The forest had grown quiet. The sound of squabbling Blue jays and the flutter of bird wings had ceased. Bright sunlight had brought out flocks and pairs of chickadees, Pine juncos, and Goldfinches; the latter now dressed in white-striped, black wings and winter olive. They had disappeared. He shivered, and noticed that clouds had moved in to obscure the sun. Shadows, which had clearly delineated the shape of each individual tree, were gone now. The resulting gray-gloom transformed the forest into a one-dimensional charcoal rendering.

The crack of a breaking twig pulled his head to the same angle as the Airedales. Donahey strained eyes and ears. The dogs leaped over the log, passing one on each side of the priest. Surprised, he fell backward, landing on his back in the snow.

Pal and Sal began to bark. A human voice shouted and yelled. Legs still hung-up on the tree trunk, Father Donahey wiggled and squirmed. His thrashing arms left the swirl patterns of half a snow angel. Using his arms to free one leg and then the other, he managed to roll over and regain his feet. About three trees deeper into the forest, the dogs circled a shadowy figure with its back up against a trunk. Donahey rushed forward, booted feet sinking into drifted snow with each step.

He skidded to a halt, slipping on ice hidden under its white cover. Donahey caught sight of short cut black hair— the man had lost his hat. The dogs bounded in and out. Dressed in Carhartt brown, bib overhauls and quilted, cotton, duck, work jacket, the stranger thrust and swung at them with an exotic weapon. What looked like a combination spear and axe heads had been fixed to a ten-foot wooden shaft.

Recognition flooded his mind.

"Jimmy. Jimmy Wong, what are you doing?"

The man glanced at the priest and grimaced. He shook the weapon. "Father, call off your dogs!"

Donahey fumble-fingered the iPad. He managed to get it clicked on and punched the recall button. Pal and Sal rushed to his side. Jimmy lifted his weapon to the vertical and approached.

The priest's memory supplied background information. The Wong family had been members of the church since the late 1930's. Jimmy's grandfather had immigrated to Winterset with Catholic missionaries to escape the Japanese invasion of China. The various generations since had farmed three hundred acres adjacent to this park. The locals, with what had initially been a racist reaction, labeled the spread the Wrong Farm. The name had stuck, but it was like calling a bald man Curly or a tall man Shorty. The Wong's were the top-rated farmers of the area. Their crops always achieved the highest yields while losing mere fractions of topsoil.

"Well, Father, I did not expect to see you," he waved a hand towards the dogs, "and your companions out here today."

"I know they allow black powder, bow, and shotgun hunting in these woods, but is there a spear season I don't know about?"

Jimmy blushed, his already tan cheeks and forehead darkening further. He shook the weapon. "Not a spear, Father. It's a *ji*."

"Come, let's sit and talk, my son."

Seated together on the walnut log, the pair shared a plastic bottle of Fiji water. Donahey prepared and lit his pipe. The dogs sat nearby. He let the silence grow. Many years listening to confessions told him the truth would only come if his parishioners spoke first. Asking questions would not get to the heart of the matter.

Jimmy looked around. He propped the *ji* against the tree trunk. His hands went to cover his face. In a muffled voice, he spoke. "Father, I need help. I am desperate. It is my daughter, Lien."

Donahey remembered Jimmy was a widower; his wife had died in childbirth twenty-five years ago. The baby girl had survived and grew to be a fine figure of a lass. She had made the varsity cross country teams in high school and at the university. Graduated valedictorian. He hadn't seen Lien recently. Her reporting job with National Public Radio kept her flying from one national and international news event to another.

He fished for more information. "I heard she was back visiting.

Jimmy clasped his hands together and pressed them against his lips. "You are one of the few who might just believe me if I say Lien is possessed by an evil spirit."

Donahey looked at his companion and the spear-axe at his side. A horrible feeling welled up. "You are surely not going to use that, that *ji* on your daughter?"

Jimmy's head jerked up, "No, Father, heaven forbid. You must help. Let me tell you what happened."

"As you might suspect, my son, I am a good listener." He

sucked on the pipe. It had gone out. Donahey pulled an old-fashioned wooden kitchen match from a side pocket of his parka and struck it into flame against the log's surface.

"In spite of the Japanese war and the later communist government my family has always managed to visit our relatives in China. Lien returned from such a visit a month ago. In the old days, the family farmed in *Guangdong* province. When the communists began the new open economic policy the province grew dramatically in both manufacturing and population. All the old village ways were lost.

"Factories, highways, and apartments were constructed on thousands of acres of land. What wasn't covered with concrete was poisoned with toxic industrial chemicals from unregulated dumping. The destruction and pressures of growth forced spirits and demons off lands they had possessed for thousands of years. The discredited priests were no longer able to placate and contain the nastiest ones.

'Wraiths and fiends are migrating, attempting to find new homes. They take possession of human bodies in order to travel."

Father Delaney placed a hand on Jimmy's back. "And how do you know Lien brought one back from her trip?"

"All the signs indicate the presence of the demon *Zhu Bajie*. In the long, long ago, he lived in heaven. Drink and lust led him to attack the beautiful Moon Goddess. When she complained, the Jade Emperor threw him down to earth to live as a human. Unfortunately, he fell into a pig pen and was reborn as a man-eating, pig demon."

"How can you be sure this is the one?"

"The pig personality manifests greed in everything: eating, drinking, and pleasures of the flesh. My daughter has gained thirty pounds in the last month. Her appetite for alcoholic drink, drugs, and sex is off the chart."

"Jimmy, I will call the Bishop. We can get exorcists."

"By the time they get here it will be too late, Father. As Zhu becomes more entrenched, his aura will affect everything for miles. Can you imagine the entire population of Winterset engaging in one massive orgy of drink and copulation around the town square?"

"Where is Lien now?" Donahey scanned the woods around them. "Is she here in the woods?"

"At the moment, she is safe. Using Skype and the Internet, I consulted with demon-chasers in the old country." Jimmy pulled a rolled-up, leather bag from inside his jacket and handed it to Donahey. "They gave me directions on how to make the *ji* and this magic bag to contain the evil one's *chi*."

The ivory-colored material of the bag felt soft and leathery to Donahey's fingers. The outside was completely covered with mystical Chinese characters. "I don't understand."

"In a group Skype, we chanted words from ancient holy books to force the demon out of Lien's body. I held the bag over her mouth and nostrils. The chants would drive Zhu's spirit out into the container. The bag containing the wraith would be air-freighted back to China, where it would be locked away."

Donahey removed the pipe and rubbed his chin. "And, it apparently didn't work."

Jimmy moaned and rocked. "I blew it, Father. The demon left her body. The bag slipped and it escaped. With the chanting, it couldn't go back into Lien. It broke out into the barnyard and possessed my prize Yorkshire boar. It's now roaming these woods."

This was new territory to Donahey. He had only participated in one exorcism. A professional had handled that 'casting out.' It had only been a lower grade spirit putting up little resistance. "So, what are you hoping to do now?"

"The elders told me, I must find and disable the creature enough to allow the bag to be secured around its muzzle.' He shook the spear-axe. "Then I will kill it. When the body dies, it must leave and be contained. Can you and your dogs help?"

Father Donahey brought a hand to his lips; brows came together. Staring into the woods, he twisted the bag in his hands. He tried to imagine the threat to his parishioners and to the population of the entire area. A vision of nude bodies writhing in heaps on the courthouse lawn came to his mind like a Hieronymous Bosch medieval painting of souls being tortured in hell.

The viewpoint in his hallucination changed, swooped lower, stopping at ground level next to one locked together couple. It was he, naked and straining on top of Clara Murphy. Skinny, age-spotted arms pulled him tight against her pillow-sized breasts. Her legs locked around his thighs.

And, somewhere among that moaning, giggling tangle of Iowans the pig-god was selecting a human for its next meal. *No, it must not be! He…we must stop it.*

Donahey wiped sweat from his forehead. "Jimmy, the three of us will help."

Maybe it was no coincidence he and the dogs happened to be in the right place at the right time. He pointed at the ancient, pattern, pole weapon. "Don't you have a rifle or shotgun we could use?"

"Lead won't damage it," Jimmy raised the *ji*, "only enchanted, cold iron." He locked eyes with Donahey. "It will be very dangerous, Father. Zhu will resist. He will try to kill and eat us."

***

The hunting party picked up the split-hoofed prints of the boar in the new snow. The dogs bounded ahead, following the scent. Even the humans' diminished noses could smell the sulfur, manure odor left by the demon's corporal body. The two men struggled to catch up.

Pal and Sal vanished from sight. Donahey pulled out the iPad and turned on the GPS tracking. The two stars marking the animals' positions curved through the woods. The trace they followed ran in a circle. He motioned to Jimmy. They cut through the woods in a diagonal to intercept the dogs and their prey.

The Airedales let out high-pitched warbling half-growls, half-whines. A sharp porcine shriek followed, loud enough to make the humans' ears hurt. The pair of hunters broke out of the trees into a small clearing.

The eight hundred pound boar squealed and chomped his tushes. Its rear end pushed safely back into a brush pile, it faced outward snapping and hooking eight-inch long curled tusks at its tormentors. Pal and Sal raced back and forth keeping the boar locked in place.

Jimmy shouted, "Christ Almighty! Father, forgive me for those words, but that demon has transformed my boar."

Donahey looked closer. Six-inch long prickly bristles covered every square inch of its black-mottled skin. The head and body were leaner and bonier. And, no domestic boar had tusks that long. It looked like a slapped together combination of all the nastiest features of African warthog, Arkansas razorback, and Siberian Wild boar. Sunken in flaps of fat, its tiny piggy eyes glared at the men and dogs. In the gray gloom, they glowed blood red.

Lines from Shakespeare's *Venus and Adonis* came to Donahey's mind. *His eyes like glow-worms shine when he doth fret; his snout digs sepulchers where'er he goes.*

"Father, we need to get it out in the open so I can get a whack at it. You and the dogs keep its attention. I'll sneak around the back and give it a poke."

"Wait a minute." Donahey commanded. He grasped his pocket cross in one hand and the haft of the *ji* in the other. "Our Father in Heaven, please bless our effort. If it is your will, give us success in defeating this denizen of Hell. Amen." He released the spear-axe and drew the sign of the cross on its metal. *"In Nomine Patris, et Filii, et Spiritus Sancti."*

An aura of rainbow-colored energy, St Elmo's fire,

enveloped the metal of the polearm. A combination of heathen Chinese and Christian blessings now powered the weapon. Jimmy hustled off. Father Donahey advanced to distract the beast. He waved the bag and shouted. Emboldened by his presence, the dogs rushed in both at once to snap and dance.

He heard a shout from behind the brush pile. "Here it comes!"

The massive boar squealed and exploded out. A twelve-inch long spear point in the anus was too much, even for a demon. Pig snout in his crotch, Donahey was lifted and tossed like a rag doll. He hit the brush pile and bounced off to land on his face. He pushed himself up. A stinging sensation, the boar had gored him on his inner right leg. Adrenaline flooded his bloodstream. The dogs howled. The boar roared. Their zigzagging, weaving bodies became an intricate dance of death. He must give the Airedales every advantage.

Donahey pulled out the iPad, touched the rifle icon and then the yes button. Pal and Sal became blurs. Long slashes appeared on the sides of the pig. Blood squirted out. Sal zipped in. A terrible high-pitched squeal came out. She danced back out of tusk range. The dog shook her head, tossing a pig ear and a strip of neck skin to one side. The two Airedales dove in again. The action froze.

Pal had Zhu's back leg clamped in his jaws. Sal had a grip on the opposite side pig jowl. They held their quivering prey still. Donahey limped forward and thrust the bag over the slobbering piggy mouth and flat-nosed nostrils. Jimmy appeared in his side vision, the *ji* raised over his head. The sickle-shaped axe portion came down. In amateur hands, the razor-sharp blade hit at an angle. The axe head bounced off the pig's skull shearing off a flap of skin four inches wide and eight inches long.

The boar reacted. It shook off the dogs. The bag slipped from Donahey's grasp, exposing snot-covered, nose holes. The axe came down again. The fine-honed cold iron found the spine where it joined the skull and chopped it in two.

A brown mist blew out of the boar's snout and burned into Father Donahey's mouth. It tasted like shit. He fell back. Inside him, the demon-spirit and his priest's soul struggled. He saw Jimmy's distorted face bend over him.

"Father, Oh God. Not you too?"

He sat up. Everything was tinted red. He tried to stand and then fell back. His right leg wouldn't work. Adrenalin had masked the pain of a long, tusk slash on the inside of his thigh. It had bled, soaking his pant leg. Liquid squished in his boot. In a dream state, he held up the iPad and pushed the Red Cross icon. Sal pushed her face in and began to lick the wound. The iPad dropped into the snow. A sudden bout of dizziness felt alien. He shuddered and let out a long series of pig-grunts.

Feelings and emotions coalesced. The demon personality took control. A ferocious, hungry emptiness welled up. The pig-man-priest began to get an erection. Its head spun around. A three-point crawl took the creature to the boar carcass. The new Zhu began to feed. Jimmy smacked it in the ribs with the pole-arm haft. Head turned. Jaws slobbered. Teeth nipped. Eyes glowed red.

Huddled in a tiny sliver of his repressed humanity, Donahey heard Jimmy say, "Forgive me Father" The flat part of the axe came down on his head.

***

The Donahey-Zhu creature woke. Hunger and the desire to kill filled him to bursting. All of the Seven Deadly sins: lust, gluttony, greed, sloth, wrath, envy, and pride raged and fought inside its bloated sack of skin. It tried to rise. The hybrid was secured to a bed by sticky silvery bandages. Flexing the body caused the frame to bounce—a random atonal drumbeat against the hardwood floor. The demon roared. The sound was muffled. Someone had secured a bag over its nose and mouth. It tossed its head, trying to dislodge the suffocating sack. No luck. It was stuck on with more of the silver tape.

The sound of group chanting from a computer speaker cut through its anger. They wanted it to come out. *No, nooo! Not again to be confined.* The pig-god bucked. Hands and feet quivered. Fingers and toes clasped and unclasped. Faster and faster. The crusted scab on the thigh wound cracked. Blood flowed. Bits of demon personality dissolved and floated out through nostrils and mouth. The priest personality inside began to pray. It was too much for Zhu.

***

Donahey lay propped up on Jimmy's bed, lips in a weak smile. An EMT worked on his leg. Sheriff Rick sat in a bentwood rocker, drinking coffee from a brightly colored Beijing Olympics souvenir mug. Jimmy sat, tight-lipped, in a spoke-backed Windsor chair brought in from the kitchen. Pal and Sal lay in the space between the two men, heads on crossed paws.

The med-tech spoke, "Father, I've finished stitching. Looks like someone stopped the bleeding and sterilized the wound. It's as clean as can be. Not sure how that could have happened. At any rate have your primary physician check it out tomorrow."

Lien walked in bearing a tray of chocolate chip cookies. She winked at the priest and provided a cover story. "We used Chinese medicine."

Donahey thought, *"And having genetically modified dogs who have coagulants and antibiotics in their saliva helps immensely."*

The tech took two cookies in passing and left the house. The room was silent until they heard the ambulance pull away, its tires crackling ice-coated gravel on the driveway.

The rocker creaked as the sheriff leaned forward. "Okay, I need to file a report. Let me get the story straight. Father, you were out exercising the dogs when you came upon Jimmy looking for his escaped boar. You decided to help him. When you two and the dogs finally cornered the pig, it went wild and attacked. Father Donahey was injured. Jimmy, you were forced to kill it."

"That's right, sheriff. The good Father was unconscious. I cut down two saplings and made a travois for the dogs to pull. Got him back to the house and called for help"

"Well, that all sounds good, except for a few strange odds and ends. For example, the boar was almost decapitated with a sharp heavy object. I'd guess an axe of some kind. Why an axe when a gun would kill from a distance and no one hurt?"

Rick pushed his Stetson to the back of his head. "Someone fed on the raw carcass. Bite marks looked like they were made with human teeth. And, we have one hell of a bump on the Father's head. A fact not consistent with the story."

Jimmy began to wiggle in his chair. Sweat beads appeared on his forehead.

The sheriff also has a secret, Donahey thought. He recalled the killing of two escaped criminals by the sheriff's alter ego, an Irish shape-shifting Pooka. He needed to talk to the sheriff alone. "Jimmy fetch the poleaxe. Lien could you get me a cup of that coffee? Smells great."

The priest waited until father and daughter had left the room. "Rick, I don't think you want to pursue this any further. Please accept my assurances that this episode is closed and there will be no further danger to anyone."

"Father, I have my duty."

"I know, my son. But you are in an excellent position to understand, as someone who has one foot in the mundane world and one in the supernatural."

Jimmy returned with the bloodied *ji.* Sheriff Rick's eyes grew wide. He sniffed. The arteries in his neck pulsed. Jimmy handed him the weapon. It almost slipped from his hand. The sheriff raised one finger and touched the blade. He jerked it back and stuck it in his mouth.

The lawman scrutinized the two men's faces. His eyebrows, cheeks, and lips relaxed. He stroked his chin. "I think I should dispose of this. It's probably illegal under Iowa law."

Father Donahey leaned back, let out his breath, and relaxed tense muscles. The sheriff had yielded to his gentle blackmail.

Donahey said, "Any further questions, sheriff?" He caught a micro-expression. For the briefest of seconds, the sheriff's face flashed black. In his eyes, frozen fire flared.

"No. I think this file is best closed." He forced a smile. "In this case, two Wongs make a right."

Donahey's brow wrinkled and he rolled his eyes. It was a groaner. So far, except for the local leprechaun, supernatural creatures had lacked even a modicum of human-style humor.

Sheriff Rick rose from the rocker. "I'll be on my way. I think I'll set up a speed trap over on east highway 92."

He nodded to Jimmy and Lien. "I always feel better after nailing a few DWI's."

Donahey blew on the coffee and took a sip. He noticed his pipe and the iPad on the bedside table.

Lien smiled and said, "Father, will you join us for dinner. We're going to have pork chops."

His stomach was still extended from the demon-forced meal in the woods. The memory made a tablespoon of vomit flutter up his esophagus. Lips squeezed together. He gulped and swallowed. "No thanks, Lien. I don't think I have it in me to ever eat pork again."

Author Bio

Dennis Maulsby is a retired bank president living in Ames, Iowa with his wife, Ruth, a retired legal secretary, and his dog Charlie, a retired CIA operative. His poems and short stories have appeared in numerous literary magazines and on National Public Radio. His book of war poetry, *Near Death/Near Life*, and a book of  short stories, *Free Fire Zone,* both published by Prolific Press won a gold medal award and a silver medal respectively from the Military Writers of America. For more information and free reads go to www.dennismaulsby.com.

Twenty Minutes

by Darren Todd

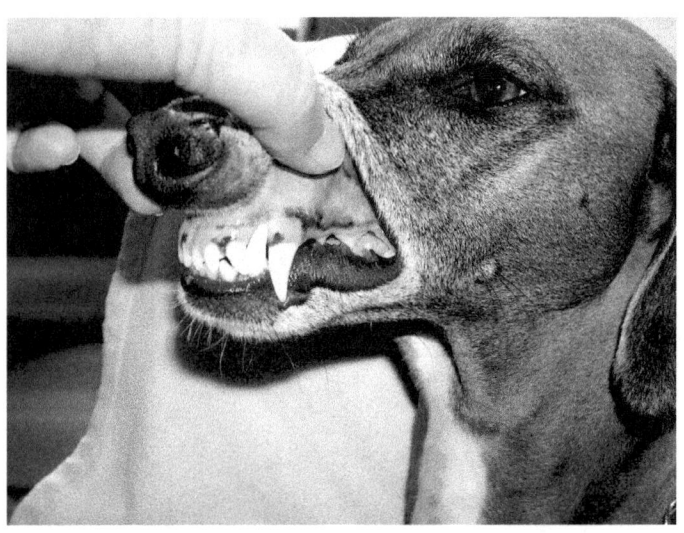

Annie's eyes fluttered open at a scraping sound and light beating down on her eyelids. Over several seconds, she registered terrible pain: her hands, her feet, especially her head.

Then panic set in. Her eyes shot open and she pulled in great gulps of air. Her feet kicked and hands flailed beneath the sheets of her bed. Not *her* bed, something smaller, higher off the ground, with plastic rails keeping her from falling to the floor. Not her *floor*, for that matter. No shag carpet here, only off-white tiles with speckles, like an egg.

Not her windows, but a single large pane with tan curtains pulled to the side, revealing a blinding white light.

Not her father and brother, but two grown men, suited and somber, rising from not-her-chairs as she flailed about.

"Where am I?" she asked them. A beeping machine attached to her arm ushered in more pain when she jerked instinctually. Pinching plastic flew from the end of her finger and the beeping moved from regular interval to steady stream.

"Calm down, ma'am," said one of the suited men. They were no angels, and this, not her heaven.

"Where am I?" she said again, and again her question remained unanswered.

In came a nurse, also ignoring her questions, who seemed interested only in her lying back down. The woman pressed a button on the side of the bed and made the back half rise.

"Just breathe," she said. "You're all right, but you won't be if you keep thrashing around."

"Where am I?" Annie asked again, this time with bite in her tone.

The nurse answered without meeting her eyes, her head still turned toward the IV in Annie's arm and the equipment beside her. "You're at Mullens Memorial Hospital. I'm your nurse, Sandy."

Sandy was maybe thirty, sturdy build. Probably hadn't seen a gym in years, but could endure a marathon if she had to.

Annie wept now, the tears coming without her understanding their origin. Then she remembered. "I was dying," she sobbed. "Am I dead?"

The nurse smiled and finally looked up at her. "No, honey, you're not dead. You're pretty banged up, but far from dead. You calm down now, all right."

"I'm Detective Heron and this is—"

"I'm sorry officers," Sandy cut them off. "That's gonna have to wait for me to take vitals and do an evaluation." She held up a finger when Detective Heron opened his mouth. "She's not going anywhere. You'll have plenty of time for that."

And so Sandy spent the next ten minutes briefing Annie, asking about her pain, explaining her meds, telling her the time, day, location.

The last Annie remembered, it was mid-morning the day before. She'd lost almost a day. Work on Friday and now here. No, something had come after starting work, but so horrible that it only appeared in short flickers and gray around the edges.

Her breathing picked up again, and the beep from her finger monitor grew more rapid.

"Keep calm," Sandy said. She turned back to the officers. "My professional opinion: this is unnecessary and probably illegal until she's been cleared by the attending physician. I'll send for him now. So I'm not gonna stop you, but you have my take on it."

Detective Heron nodded, saying nothing. He and his partner remained standing as if only waiting for Sandy to leave.

She turned back to Annie. "I'll get Dr. Hanson. He'll be along shortly. You buzz if you need anything."

Annie wanted to thank her, but she only managed a nod.

Detective Heron closed the door after Sandy. "So, as I was saying, I'm Detective Heron and this is Deputy Detective Jamison. We're from the Farraday Police Department.

"You know what happened?" Annie asked. The flickers had begun to form a narrative in her mind's eye, but she pushed it to the background. If she focused on those images too long, she'd lose her mind.

Heron bobbed his head side to side. He was lanky. Beneath a thin jacket, he wore a button-up tucked into slacks with no more than a twenty-eight inch waist. He was fortyish, dour, and looked at the floor more than he made eye contact. Thick hair without a hint of baldness had nonetheless turned a dark gray, and he let it stand on his head with no effort at style. "We know some," he said. "That's why we're here. We're hoping you can help us with the rest."

She shook her head and looked up at the lights. One of the halogen bulbs ticked, threatening to go out. "I don't know how much I remember. It's coming back, but only flashes."

"Flashes work," said the other, the deputy detective, whatever that meant. He was dumpier, almost chubby beside Heron. Near the same age, his face seemed friendlier. He took off his tweed jacket and placed it on the back of his chair. He wore a button-up as well, but his was striped, daddish. He wore a tie, tethered to his shirt with a nickel-sized pin of a dog. A Great Dane, maybe?

"I thought I was dead," she said, her tone flat.

"We got that from Doctor Cannode," Heron said, eyes on the floor, hands on his hips.

"He's okay?" Annie asked. The meter again picked up the pace and revealed her excitement. She wanted to pull it off her finger, but thought that might make Sandy angry.

"He is," Jamison said. "Woke maybe two hours ago to about the same reaction as you."

"Are we the only survivors?" she asked. She looked down at the light blue blanket of her bed.

"Nope," Jamison said. "Everyone made it. They all survived."

Something like excitement passed through her, then confusion. Her mouth seemed unable to choose an expression and twitched instead. She sucked in her lips to calm herself. "I thought we were dying. We all did."

Heron shrugged. "That seems to be the consensus. But we're gonna need a little more than that."

More images filled her mind, of arms and legs and cages. "He was a big man," she blurted. "Really big. As silly as it sounds, I thought of one of those wrestlers from TV. Only he dressed normal. He had on a black shirt, and—"

"We have Jeremy Bider in custody, ma'am," Heron said. He looked up finally and raised his eyebrows. "He turned himself in not a half hour after… all that happened. He's confessed already. Booked. Processed." The detective made an odd clapping gesture with one palm across the other, as if a rock skipping along the surface of a pond.

Her head filled with questions, but none she could knit into a cohesive sentence. "How… I mean… why question me then? I don't understand."

"This wasn't the only attack," Jamison said. "Your lab was one of ten." He held up his splayed fingers in case she'd forgotten the number.

"And we're damn sure that in each case, there was someone on the inside," Heron said.

The monitor again betrayed her apprehension, and again she teetered on tearing the finger sensor off. "If you think I had something to do with that… horror, then you're wasting your time and mine." She couldn't help it, more tears came.

The detectives waited, as if prepared for any number of breakdowns, but still with a bevy of questions and accusations in their queue.

When she quieted, Jamison slouched and threw up his arms. "Look, we only want your side of the story. We're not accusing anyone of anything other than Bider himself. So take your time, and start from the beginning. That morning. Yesterday morning, from when you got to work."

Annie wiped her cheeks and slowed her breathing. She

closed her eyes to the light and thought back to the previous morning, which to her seemed like only hours and yet a lifetime ago.

"I went to work at the usual time, maybe a couple minutes after, 'cause I stopped for coffee, which I do maybe twice a week. Dr. Cannode doesn't care about being there to the minute because we don't really start processing the animals till about nine."

"What about before then?" Heron asked.

"Just prep work, which for me means checking the tanks, the cages, and whatever is scheduled that day. The chambers aren't the only thing I do. I've just made it the most important thing. Otherwise, it just gets… sloppy, kinda like it was before I got there."

Heron pulled a notebook from his pocket and consulted it. "You've been there for six months. Right. So who did you replace?"

"They'd hire itinerant workers. Recent immigrants, I guess. And they'd take care of disposal, but they weren't doing it very well. I mean, they were fast and good workers and all, but they didn't care."

"And you care?" Jamison asked, almost a statement. He held out an open hand as if ushering in her words.

"I mean, yeah. To them, it was just a job. Was, is, I guess, since there's still Dmitri who's full-time and we get Marcos who comes in on Thursdays and Fridays when our workload's a little heavier and we clean out the burners."

"The burners?" Heron asked.

"The incinerators. They fill up with ash pretty quickly,

so we empty them at the end of the week."

Heron shrugged, wrote something down, and then gestured for her to continue.

"So anyway, I came in normal time, a bit after, whatever. We started prep work, and I remember drinking my coffee—I got a latte. I normally get a breve, but changed it up for some reason. So we're working, I'm drinking. Then…." She stopped and shook her head. What had been a natural delay to swallow and take a breath extended for several, long seconds. She felt the detectives' eyes on her, heavy and expectant. She laughed without humor, and it turned into a cry.

"Then I woke up in a cage."

"Hold on," Heron said. "You're drinking your morning coffee. It's not yet nine. No animals yet. So what happened between the coffee and waking up in the cages? You felt dizzy? You fell asleep? You dropped to the floor?"

She looked to the ceiling, squinting into the light. "I don't remember any of that. I was prepping with Dmitri. When I woke up, I was hunched over in a cage. I couldn't move—"

"You were sedated?" Jamison prodded.

"I couldn't move in the cage. It's meant for a medium-sized dog. I had my knees against my chest, could barely breathe…."

"How long before Bider comes around?"

Annie closed her eyes to the image of Bider walking past the cages—no hurry, no fuss, just doing a job, and it sent a shiver through her. "A few minutes. Long enough for everyone to wake up. He'd put me beside the custodian, Mr. Tuttle."

"James Tuttle," Heron read from his journal. "Three cracked ribs, mild concussion, multiple contusions and lacerations."

"He fought," Annie said. "He's older." She frowned, holding back more tears. "He reminds me of my dad. But he was banging on the cage and then he tried to fight when that animal took him."

"Jeremy Bider," Heron said, as if confirming who she meant.

She nodded. "He was the only one. The others must have told you that. Mr. Tuttle fought back, and so did some of the others, but it didn't matter. That... Bider, he threw them around like they were just... meat. He used a guide pole, and—"

Heron held up a hand. "A guide pole?"

Annie gesticulated as best she could with one arm IVed and her finger trapped in a sensor. "It's for looping around the dog's neck so you can... guide it along."

"To the chambers," Jamison finished.

Annie nodded.

"He used them on... most of us, not just the ones who resisted."

"The same ones you use on the dogs," Jamison said. Something in his tone sounded goading, and she involuntarily winced, like his words had pinched her.

"*I* didn't. I mean, almost never. Dmitri and Marcos, sometimes. Too much, really, but I got them to handle the animals with more... finesse."

Jamison chuckled. "But why bother? They're on their way across the Rainbow Bridge, right?"

Annie closed her eyes at another pinch. "Yes, they are, but it's also an end to their suffering. There's no reason to make it worse. No reason to handle them... like Bider handled us." She set her jaw and stared Jamison down.

If he cared, he never showed it. Just shrugged and went back to his tiny notepad. A little leather model, much nicer than Heron's Dollar Store version.

Heron stepped forward, as if separating a school yard scuffle. "So he used the guide poles. Okay. We know that. The thing that bothers me is that he's able to get in there and sedate a lab full of people without so much as a raising a cry for help. No alarm, no cell phone call to 911 or a panicked call to a spouse. Not even a text."

"He took our phones. We're not supposed to have them on in the lab anyway, but I keep mine on vibrate. I'm away from the clean room, so it doesn't really matter. But he took all of them."

Heron scrunched his face. The gesture seemed genuine, not an affectation, like he was actually racking his brains to piece the scene together. "Sure, he took 'em. I get that. But they didn't magically jump into his pocket, and none of you entered the cages willingly, I'm assuming. So a total stranger, a guy as big as a pro wrestler, like you say, comes into your secure facility and cages eight people without so much as a Tweet going up in alarm."

Jamison shook his head. Annie liked him less and less.

"Someone must have let him in," Annie said, and both detectives lit up, eyes moving to meet hers.

"That's what we concluded, as well," Heron said.

"Someone let him in. Someone who knew what was going to happen. I saw the video files. The old files, I mean. The tapes of Bider's attack are conveniently missing. You guys have one of those…." He drew out the word, snapping his fingers.

"Anterooms," Jamison chimed in.

"Yeah, that's right. An anteroom. The door opens on one end, there's a room in between where security can verify who's who and all that, and then they have to buzz a second door to let someone in. Is that right?"

Annie remained quiet for several seconds. "You… you'll have to talk to security about that. I mean, yes, there's an anteroom, but it's not like what you said."

"Do tell," Jamison said. He was looking at his fingernails, clicking the thumbnail against the others.

"That's how it's supposed to work. But most mornings," she signed. A lump formed in her throat as a mental picture of George—the chubby and affable head of security—danced through her mind. "Most mornings, they just open the second door and let us through. I mean, the reader captures a snapshot of our access anyway, and we all know each other, so it's not a big deal."

"They," Jamison said. He looked up at her pursed his lips. "Who's 'they'?"

"Our security guy is George Streffan. But it's not like it was his idea."

"Was it yours?" Jamison asked.

She shook her head, looked down to calm what was quickly turning into a tight knot in her stomach. She lay back in bed. At least the pain seemed to ease up a bit, either from her meds or her anger at this interrogation. "This was all going on when I got there six months ago." She looked up and tilted her head. "And I think you already know that."

Heron held up a hand. "All right. So he takes you out of the cage."

"Yes. After Mr. Tuttle."

"Then what?"

"The chambers."

"The gas chambers," he said.

Just the name made her shudder. Her jaw quivered, and she had to open and close it several times to stop the spasm. "Yes, the gas chambers."

"Pretend I know nothing," he said. "Walk me through it. This is where you work. You do this every day, and from what it sounds like, you're damn good at it. So just think about it like a normal day, as odd as that sounds, and talk us through. Take as long as you need."

She pulled in a deep breath, closed her eyes, and spoke. "I'm like Temple Grandin. You know her? She's the autistic lady who consults for slaughter houses. Well, she discovered that the whole process was breaking down right on the kill floor. The cows are dumb, sure, but they knew what was coming, and they got scared."

"What does this have to do with—" Jamison said.

"Shut up, deputy detective, and listen. It's important. So she designs curved chutes so the cows can't see what's coming, so they don't get so scared…." She started crying now, couldn't help it. "And a restraint system that kept them still for the deathblow. The whole thing worked better. The cows died a more peaceful death, fewer injuries, smoother throughput, everybody wins."

"And that's what you do for the animals at your facility," Heron said.

Annie nodded, eyes still closed. Darkness but for the glow of light from the window, made crimson through her eyelids. "I made those poor… those animals' final minutes a little more peaceful. You jack them around with those goddamn guide poles and they go into the chambers fighting and frightened. It's pretty terrible. I gave them… dignity and even love in their last seconds on Earth, and that makes all the difference. We finished our work faster, fewer injuries, greater efficiency, all because of me."

"So that's why Bider took it easy on you?" Jamison said, tone no longer *hinting* but outright accusing now.

"You call this easy?" she yelled and pointed at her face. "You call getting crammed into the same tiny boxes you've used to kill thousands of animals and getting the same gas pumped in, knowing—absolutely knowing—you're gonna die, easy?"

"Unless you knew you *weren't* gonna die," Jamison said.

"Go fuck yourself," she barked.

"But he did spare you the pole," Heron interrupted. "No marks around the neck. He didn't use the pole on you."

She calmed a bit. "No, but he didn't on a couple others, either."

"Why?" Heron asked.

"No idea. You have him in custody. He sounds

cooperative enough. You'll have to ask him."

"So the gas chambers," Heron said, making a carry-on gesture with his free hand.

"It takes them twenty minutes to die." Tears again, pouring now. "It's not like euthanasia. For twenty goddamn minutes they're stuffed in those crates, just hoping that maybe it will end, that someone will come rescue them. Until everything goes black and *that's* their rescue. I made sure they didn't lose hope. I was putting them to sleep. I wasn't killing them."

Heron cleared his throat. "So he didn't use the pole on you."

"This again? Do I look like a threat to you?"

Jamison huffed. "Mr. Tuttle looks about as intimidating as my grandfather, but Bider slung him around like a rag doll, Ms. Nolen."

"You're wasting your time," she said.

"How's that, Annie?" Heron asked.

"We had two people absent yesterday. One of them has only worked there a month. Rich something. Works in R and D. And Jerry Porter, our vendor. He's supposed to be there for the head injury mapping tests. He'd been called away, so we weren't going to do the mapping that day. You might want to start with them."

Heron flipped through his notebook, though Annie got the feeling he knew everything that lay on those pages already. "We spoke to both of them, though I appreciate the information. They came forward right away. Very cooperative. Richard Schoop worked at the post office until his branch closed about a month ago."

"That proves nothing," she snapped. "Just like Bider not kicking the shit out of me proves nothing."

"Do you stand by your lab's work?" Jamison asked. He moved to the chair and sat, pulled a Styrofoam cup from the floor to his lips and sipped.

"What do you mean?"

He shrugged. "Your lab kills what, five thousand canines a year for product testing? You all right with that?"

She huffed. "You should do your homework. Product testing is one part. There's trauma research, medical implants. Life saving work being done there. We don't just test shampoos."

He shrugged again. "My mistake. I'm just saying' that you seem pretty sympathetic to the dogs." He held up his tie pin, the shirt stretching out. "I've got a dog myself. Great Dane. Apollo. He's a mess," Jamison laughed "but I don't know what I'd do without him. Can't stand the idea that some lab would put him through hell and then gas him and burn him just so—what?—so we know a little bit more about how a human might react to some drug?"

She sniffed and shook her head. "You sound pretty sympathetic yourself. Where were you yesterday morning?"

He laughed, but no humor lined the sound as it banked off the walls.

"Besides, we don't use Great Danes."

He frowned in mock contemplation. "What do you use? Strays?"

"Beagles. Farmed Beagles, mostly."

"How come?"

Annie closed her eyes. "Cause they don't bite. No matter what you do to them, they won't bite you."

Jamison shook his head. "That's pretty messed up. The idea of that."

"There are rules, and we follow them."

Heron piped up. "What was it like in there? In the gas chambers."

The name again drove a spike of anxiety into her skull. "Horrifying. The chambers are sealed, but we're all aware of how that stuff smells. And that's what Bider pumped in. I don't know what he actually used to knock us out, but he must have made sure it smelled the same. I was scared the whole time, sure, but a part of me still hung on to hope, even when he threw us into the chambers. Like he'd stop there. He *had* too, or he'd kill all of us and turn some protest into mass murder. So I figured he was some fanatic wanting to prove a point and he'd lock us into the chambers until someone came to let us out. When the gas came on and I smelled it, that medicinal stink, I panicked."

"So you go in there thinking maybe things are gonna be okay. Terrible, sure, but you'll live," Heron said.

"Right," Jamison jumped on board. "Maybe that's why you didn't fight back, saved yourself the pain of having a guide pole around your neck, maybe a few broken bones. One guy's larynx was all but crushed. You don't need that kinda pain, not if you think you're gonna live through it."

A tear fell on Annie's hand. She only then noticed she'd started up again. The lump in her throat felt like a physical thing, eager to leave her body, like if she retched over the side of the bed, some vital part of her would fall to the floor.

"I guess so," she said, finally.

The detectives moved closer. She could feel their eyes on her, but she kept staring at her hands.

"Care to know what happened at the other facilities?" Heron asked.

She shook her head, but said, "Not the same thing?"

"'Fraid not, though maybe you guys got the worst of it. Nothing to brag about, I guess. A testing facility outside of Boston was breeched at the same time. Same hour, even. The guy restrains the whole staff and administers a... what did they call it?" he asked Jamison.

Jamison rifled through his notes. "An LD50," he said.

"Right. That's where—"

"I know what it is," she said. "They test a cocktail that they believe will kill half of the subjects. Lethal Dose, Fifty Percent. LD50."

Heron whistled. "Pretty terrible stuff."

"But those take time," she said.

"Not this one," said Jamison. "The guy tells 'em he's cooked up an accelerated batch. The whole staff watches as one by one half of them 'die'. I mean, none actually died. He used a barbiturate. Doses the doctor first so no one's the wiser watching this all go down. Horrible."

She looked up and found something close to genuine concern on Heron's face. Jamison was cleaning his teeth with his tongue. "What about the other places?" she asked.

"There was a head trauma department in Ohio got hit. The guys there—two of 'em, this time—they put all the staff in traction. When the staffers wake up, the two guys tell 'em *they* were tested this time, with those machines that," he twitched his head "that jerk the animals' head to the side like that. But the attackers had performed an epidermal on the staffers, so none of 'em can feel their legs. Then the attackers tell them the process had paralyzed them. Even showed 'em video, all the machines turned down you understand. Nothing that actually hurt them. It was for effect."

"My God," Annie wept.

"Guess it worked," Jamison said. PD there said they'd never seen anything like it. One guy even bit his tongue off trying to kill himself."

"Jesus."

Heron walked over to the bed and put a hand on hers. "In every case—all ten—the perps slid through there easy as butter. They all turned themselves in. No fight. No fuss. But somebody helped them. And not just with a stolen badge or something. The facilities all had redundant security. It took an insider to make it happen that smoothly."

He leaned down. "These guys that turned themselves in." He shook his head. "They'll get life or damn near it, even if nobody died. But you think they care?" He shook his head, a frown creasing his face, dimpling his chin. "They finished their job, and now they get a lifetime of media attention. Book deals, interviews, fan mail." He blew through his nose. "It's the insiders that worry me."

She bit. "What do you mean?"

He squeezed lightly on her arm and gave it a pat. He leaned in even closer and softened his voice. "Way I see it, they got the raw deal here. Say they agreed to help these guys. They let 'em in, maybe to free the animals, make a political statement, whatever. They don't know the score, no way. Don't know that to prove their own innocence, they gotta go through all that." He pointed out the window, but the effect manifested the horrors of all of the other facilities in her mind. She'd only been working there for six months, but she'd learned enough about animal testing to know that if someone wanted to use their work as torture, it wouldn't be hard to come up with creative ideas.

"But if the insiders knew they weren't gonna die..." Annie said.

"Nah, no way," Heron all but whispered. "They can't have known. Even that's too much trust. To great a chance of exposing the ruse. They lined up the insiders same as all the others. Left high and dry by the very ideologues who needed them the day before. You know what that kind of betrayal must feel like?"

He looked at Annie, warm, caring compassion lining his face.

"Detective Heron," she said.

He patted her hand again. "I know. Just let me help you."

She opened her mouth to speak when the door swung open.

"Not a word," barked a suited man. He pointed to Annie as if flagging her for execution.

"Who the hell—" Jamison said, but the suited man kept his eyes on Annie.

"I'm Kyle Hallow from Gentry, Gommel, and Morris. I

represent Falstaff Laboratories and all its employees. Ms. Nolen, don't say another word. What these gentlemen failed to tell you was that you could have a lawyer present during any questioning, and that you were free to stop this at any time. Somehow I think that part was omitted."

Detective Heron held up his hands. "We're just having a conversation, counselor."

Mr. Hallow pursed his lips. "Not any more. My client will be happy to make a formal statement once she's of sound mind and body. She's been through a living nightmare, and I don't feel that now is the time to solicit information."

Heron turned back to Annie. "He's not your buddy. He's here to provide counsel so you don't sue the lab. Nothing more."

"Good day, detectives," Kyle said. "I'll take your contact info on your way out."

Heron dug into his back pocket and pulled out a stained, leather card holder. He produced the card, but instead of handing it to her lawyer, he put it into Annie's hand.

"I look forward to getting the rest of your side of the story. With or without counsel."

She nodded, but then looked away.

"Good day, Ms. Nolen," Jamison said, sans Heron's manufactured warmth.

"Detective," she called.

Kyle Hallow held up a hand and gave her a stern look.

"I hope that when Apollo crosses the Rainbow Bridge, you're there for him."

His face lost some of its smug expression. "I will be.

'Course now he'll have to wait in line. You know how many dogs are gonna get the juice now that animal testing is all but history? Bet Bider never thought of that."

"Enough," Kyle said. He smoothed out the air in front of him with parting, open palms and rolled his shoulders forward.

Annie wanted to keep quiet, but twenty-four hours ago, she thought she was going to die. "Twenty minutes," she reminded Jamison. "We breed them in cages, we torture them, and then we throw them into a box where they spend the last twenty minutes of their lives knowing they're dying."

"They don't know," Jamison said, the quake of emotion surfacing.

"All they've known from us is torture. We created their hell on earth. What else would they expect from us?"

With that, the detectives left. Annie and Kyle sat in silence until the last of the heel beats from the hallway tapered off.

Author Bio

Darren writes short fiction full time, along with freelance book editing for Evolved Publications and narrating the occasional audiobook for Audible, Inc. His short fiction has appeared in twenty-eight publications over the last twelve years. He has had four plays produced and a non-fiction book published.

His style and reading preferences tend toward the psychological, as he enjoys stories that linger in the imagination long after he's closed the book on them.

He lives in Scottsdale, Arizona with his wife and son, and does his best work in coffee shops on a dated word processor. darrentodd.net

www.ingramcontent.com/pod-product-compliance
Lightning Source LLC
Chambersburg PA
CBHW072052170626
46813CB00004B/1316